Praise for
THE WRONG SHOES

'A sobering, thoughtful and ultimately powerful
novel about a brave young man moving forwards
despite his difficult circumstances.'
THE BOOKSELLER

'Every chapter is full of experience &
empathy & most importantly, heart.'
PHIL EARLE

'Reading fiction is about walking in the shoes of people
whose lives are very different to ours and allowing more
readers to see themselves in stories. *The Wrong Shoes* is the
perfect example of both – the right book at the right time.'
TOM PALMER

'A superbly courageous and timely book.
Will is a protagonist so many children and adults
will identify with, really beautiful.'
STEVEN LENTON

'A brilliant book – such a perfect marriage of words and
illustrations and an important story told with real heart.'
CHRISTOPHER EDGE

'An extraordinary, powerful and moving
book that has the potential to change lives.'
HANNAH GOLD

'A hopeful, honest, big-hearted read. You'll be rooting
for the main character, Will, from the very first page . . .'
CLARA VULLIAMY

'A beautifully illustrated, deeply moving,
empathy-boosting story . . .'
RASHMI SIRDESHPANDE

THE WRONG SHOES

THE WRONG SHOES

TOM PERCIVAL

SIMON & SCHUSTER

First published in Great Britain in 2024 by Simon & Schuster UK Ltd

1 3 5 7 9 10 8 6 4 2

Simon & Schuster UK Ltd
1st Floor, 222 Gray's Inn Road
London
WC1X 8HB

www.simonandschuster.co.uk
www.simonandschuster.com.au
www.simonandschuster.co.in

Simon & Schuster Australia, Sydney
Simon & Schuster India, New Delhi

A CIP catalogue record for this book is available from the British Library.

HB ISBN 978-1-3985-2712-6
eBook ISBN 978-1-3985-2715-7
eAudio ISBN 978-1-3985-2713-3

Typeset in the UK by Sorrel Packham

Printed and bound in the UK
using 100% renewable electricity
at CPI Group (UK) Ltd

MIX
Paper | Supporting
responsible forestry
FSC® C171272
www.fsc.org

This book is dedicated to
anyone who's ever felt a bit like Will.

ACT ONE

CHAPTER ONE

THIS IS NO FAIRY TALE.

Not unless it's one of those *really* old-fashioned ones, where basically a whole load of terrible stuff happens to some poor unsuspecting kid. I guess I should count myself lucky that a wolf hasn't dressed up like my nan and tried to eat me yet. But you know what? Even then, even in those stories where people get ripped in half, chewed up and spat out, *eventually* there's a happy ending. And that's the difference, see? Because this is just my life, and *nothing's* guaranteed.

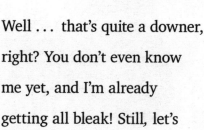

Well ... that's quite a downer, right? You don't even know me yet, and I'm already getting all bleak! Still, let's start as we mean to go on, as my dad would say.

So I guess we might as well start here, and what do you know? It's raining. I mean, no surprise, right? Of *course* it's raining, just to make my day that little bit worse. Let me explain ... There's a split in the sole of my shoe, right on the ball of my foot, like a little mocking mouth that opens and closes each time I take a step.

And what does that mean when it rains? You've guessed it – it means a wet foot!

And who likes having a wet foot? You're absolutely correct – *nobody*!

I mean, I know that things could be worse, and you've got to have a sense of proportion, but, even so, a cold, wet foot can get you down pretty quickly. So that's STRIKE ONE against my shoes – they let water in, which is pretty much a fundamental *no-no* as far as I'm concerned. But even when they were brand new, and didn't leak at all, they were *still* horrible. They were *always* wrong.

Dad says we can probably make them last until the end of the year, so long as I don't grow any more. I think that was one of his jokes – but it's hard to say. It used to be easy to tell when Dad was joking – his eyes would light up, and so would I – everything would feel warm and we'd both laugh – you know, *properly* laugh.

That doesn't happen so much now.

Either way, these are my shoes, and there's no way round it. Still, on the plus side, I don't need to worry about anyone stealing them – who'd want them?

So I'm hurrying through the rain, hoping to get to

school as quickly as possible. I suppose that makes me sound all super academic – but it's more that it's warm and dry there, and, I tell you what, it's pretty much winter now and our flat is freezing!

So this is what I do every morning (apart from weekends and the holidays *obviously*) – I drag myself out of bed, through the door and off to school. Sometimes I meet up with Cameron along the way. He's my best friend and lives across town – but it might as well be a whole other world really – a world of nicely painted doors, big gardens and Land Rovers parked on the driveway.

But, on this particular morning, I don't see Cameron – I don't see anyone. Well, no one that I want to – although I *do* see Chris Tucker. He's pretty much the worst. Some kids seem to like him, or pretend to like him, or whatever. I think they're just scared of him, to be honest.

He started going to the gym in town a while back, even though he's only in the year above me, so still too young to be *meant* to go. But his brother knows the guy who runs the gym, and if people are scared of Chris, then I don't even know the word for how they'd feel about his brother. Basically he's not someone that you say 'no' to – not if you like the way your face looks.

So now Chris walks around with his chest all puffed out and his arms swinging out from his body, like his muscles are *so* big he can't hold his arms by his sides any more (they're not, and he could), but none of that really matters, because even though his muscles aren't actually *mega* big, he's still pretty hard – *definitely* harder than me – and he knows it.

Chris *loves* to have a little chat with me. I'm, like, one of his favourite people because he can rip it out of me for my shoes, my coat, my bag, whatever. We're *so tight* he's even got a nickname for me, which him and his 'mates' think is the funniest thing ever.

As soon as I see him on the road, I put my headphones on and turn the music up so I can pretend not to have noticed him. It seems to have worked until I feel the headphones pulled off my ears.

'Hey, Poundland,' he says, lips curling up in a grin, 'what's going on?'

'Oh, hey, Chris. Nothing really, just . . . you know . . . going to school.'

'Well, *durr*!' he says.

I shrug and try to put my headphones back on, but Chris keeps hold of them.

'So you been doing those doodles again –' Chris nods at the designs I've drawn on my bag in marker pen; a fat smile snakes across his face as he finishes his sentence – 'Doodler?'

This is what Chris does. He's like a fisherman waiting by the river, casting out his line, trying to get a bite so he can reel you in. He's only saying that to get a rise out of me, but do you know what? It doesn't work – I'm actually proud of *that* nickname.

A couple of years ago, I got into the local paper for doing some pictures on the wall of a cafe. It was owned by this woman called Sally, a friend of my mum's. She'd seen my drawings round at ours one evening and asked me to do some doodles outside the bathrooms in her cafe. Lots of people liked them, and she asked me to do some more in the main cafe. In the end I pretty much covered a whole wall! I remember we all went out one night – me, Dad and Mum, all together – for the big unveiling. That was when someone from the paper took the photo of me in front of the wall and christened me the Doodler. Lots of kids used to call me that for a while.

That feels like a long time ago and the cafe's closed now. It's a shame. Sally used to give me free drinks whenever I went in. Tell you what, I could really do with *that* right now.

'Come on, I bet you've got *something* to show off,' presses Chris. 'You're always scribbling away. Let's have a look!'

'Give it a rest,' I say. 'It's hammering down! I'm not getting my sketchbook out here.'

'I just want a *look*,' he says, hands raised in a shrug, making out like he's being totally reasonable.

'Leave it out, I don't want to be late for school.'

'Fair enough, *goody-goody*.'

And that's it. Chris lets go of my headphones and steps aside, letting me walk past. I breathe a small, silent sigh of relief.

Moments later, I feel a sharp tugging on my back as he yanks the bag off my shoulder. Dad's always on at me to wear my bag with both straps across my back. For once I wish that I did.

'Get off!' I shout.

'Ooh, *feisty*!' replies Chris in a sing-song voice.

'Seriously, get lost, all right?' I try to grab my bag, but Chris laughs as he holds my arm back. Like I said, he's not massive or anything but what I *didn't* say is just how skinny *I* am.

'What is *that*?'

Chris has pulled out my sketchbook and is holding it open with one hand. I watch as blunt bullets of rain explode across my drawing. Ink pools, and then runs down the paper as the picture of a dragon, which is curled across the pages, bleeds and runs. The ferocity I gave the dragon while I was drawing it is meaningless

now – the powerful figure riding on its back is dressed in chainmail that's useless against the rain. A moment later, the dragon's sharp fierce eye is obliterated by

the rain dripping off the edge of Chris's cap.

'You're a secret Dungeons and Dragons nerd?' he says. 'That is SO . . . well, so *typical*, I guess!'

He tosses my sketchbook back towards me. I totally miss it, *obviously*, and it lands on the thin patch of grass by the pavement.

As I'm bending down to pick it up, he pushes me slightly with his foot; it's not even a shove really, just enough to knock me off balance and I fall forward.

'See you in school, Poundland,' he calls as he walks off.

See what I mean? Chris Tucker is the *worst*.

CHAPTER TWO

TO BE HONEST, THE WHOLE CHRIS thing didn't bother me too much. I get a good bit of stick from most people. I mean, most people don't *actually* push me about. But pretty much everyone rips it out of me. Mainly because of the shoes.

Okay, here we go again – the shoes . . .

I guess I should describe them. Well, that's easy – they're ugly. Just plain ugly. Plastic leather, cheap, nasty. Everyone else has Stan Smiths or black Nikes or Reebok classics or something, and the other kids who wear actual *shoe* shoes have got ones that look, you know, *decent*. But mine cost just under a tenner and they look like it too.

So, yeah, I'm used to the ribbing. Doesn't mean I *like* it – but I'm used to it.

I hadn't zipped my bag up after Chris grabbed it, so when I fell, everything burst out of it like the world's most disappointing firework and scattered across the pavement. It took me ages to scoop it all up, and in the end I had to sprint to make it to school on time. So now I'm sitting here, soaking wet, kind of puffing and gasping.

The head's sat up there at the front of the stage with all the other teachers lined up either side of him. Like he's the general of this bland middle-aged army. The same thing happens every time the head does an assembly. He greets us, then walks over to the far side of the hall to put on some dramatic music that is meant to inspire us all to greatness or something.

The head always shuts his eyes to 'appreciate' the music, but I think he just has a quick nap. He's been doing the same thing for *years*. I know because Mum's bloke, Greg, went to the same school and the head was there even way back *then* doing *exactly* the same thing.

So, anyway, the music finishes, the head nods to himself, then stands up to deliver the important news.

As per usual, it's all about the kids who've been excelling at this, flourishing in that and *striving for magnificence* in the other. So we all get to sit back and listen to how Evie Smith's been selected for the county championships in judo, how Naomi Zhao who used to go to our school has won some award for setting up a renewable energy business even though she's only eighteen, and how David Forrester's just passed his Grade Seven flute exam. Then we all do a big celebratory clap for them all together.

I mean, *personally*, I think I'd want a bit of the glory just for me and not to have to share it – but that's not really an issue, because it's not like it's EVER going to happen. Not unless the head's going to suddenly start giving out awards for *most items of essential school equipment not brought in during a week.*

So I'm sat there clapping, but there's a big part of me that's not clapping.

Well, to be honest, it's *most* of me that's not clapping. The only bits that are clapping are the palms of my hand, right? But, joking aside, the thing is, do you know *why* all these kids are good at this stuff?

And yeah, of course it's practice. Of *course* it's hard work. I'm not saying that Evie doesn't live, sleep, breathe, eat and drink judo – she does, and, fair play, she'd make mincemeat out of me and pretty much anyone else who stepped up to her – but how do you *get* to practise this stuff? How do you get *taught*? A lot of the time it's all extra – *extra* tuition, *extra* clubs at the weekend, *extra* time going to matches and practices, *extra* focus from your folks – extra *money*.

Remember I mentioned Cameron earlier, right? Cameron Romelle? He's one hundred per cent my best friend and has been for forever, really. We came up from the same primary and I can't remember a time that we weren't friends. Anyway, he plays the violin and, I tell you what, he is *amazing*! To listen to him play is just . . . well . . . it's like you're floating along on a river of music or something – *seriously* it's something else. But the thing is, I know full well he has two lessons a week. And they're not cheap. I mean, like I say, I love to hear Cameron play. I'd *love* to be able to play like that – I love music generally – but you can't eat it.

We're done with the clapping now. The head rambles on about some other stuff, but I kind of zone out and the next thing I know we're all filing out of the hall and Cameron's running up towards me, his face lit up like Christmas and he's zipping his bag open, reaching inside to pull something out.

MATE! Just wait until you see these BAD BOYS!

CHAPTER THREE

You know when you're really surprised by something? Like, completely, *genuinely* shocked? That sudden gasp of breath, as if you've just smashed through thin ice on a frozen river and your body temperature drops several degrees.

Well, that *isn't* the feeling I get when Cameron shows me his new trainers.

They're these limited-edition black and gold Nikes he had sent over from Japan. He was showing me them online when I was round at his the other day.

And, yeah, they're nice – *really* nice – but *seriously* they cost *loads*. Probably more than my dad would bring home in over a month – even when he *had* a job. Cameron's been on about them for a while now, saying how great they were, but he didn't know if he'd be allowed to get them as his parents wanted him to save up for them, so that he'd . . . *understand the value of money.*

Now, don't get me wrong, I like Cameron's folks. I really do. They always chat to me when I go round, and genuinely seem to listen to what I'm saying, but *seriously* . . . that line about wanting Cameron to *understand the value of money*? I mean, *come on*! If Cameron expressed a passing interest in astronomy, they'd be buying him an observatory! So I *knew* it was just a matter of time before those trainers popped up.

'See that bit?' asks Cameron, pointing at a flexible panel on the side of his trainers, 'it's a screen! Check it out, you can customise it too. Look, I'll show you, *say cheese*!' Taking out his phone, Cameron snaps a shot of me, taps a few buttons in an app, bumps up the contrast, pings them over on Bluetooth, and then, seconds later, there's my startled-looking face peering out from behind the gold tick on the side of his trainers.

'Pretty sweet, right?'

'Pretty sweet!' I agree, clapping him on the back.

I mean, what can you do? He's *well* excited, and I'm not about to rain all over his picnic. Besides, it's not Cameron's *fault* that he gets all this stuff – just like it's not my *fault* that I don't. It's just the way things are.

'So you still coming over tonight?' he asks.

'Let me check my diary . . .' I say, pulling out an imaginary book and pretending to flick through the pages. 'Yes,' I say eventually. 'You'll be *pleased* to hear that tonight is, in fact, free.'

Cameron grins. His easy-going nature does what it always does and thaws me a little bit, softens some of my harder edges and makes me feel like a normal person again.

We'll have a laugh later. I know we will. We'll keep building that game we've been making online, and his dad will have sorted something *amazing* out for tea. Cameron's dad LOVES food. He runs this company selling smoked salmon, smoked ham, smoked cheese and smoked ANYTHING. Seriously, I'd be surprised if he wasn't working on a way to make smoked jelly and ice cream.

Cameron looks over my shoulder and his face suddenly drops.

'All right, losers?' calls Chris Tucker as he strolls over, shoulders rolling left to right, as Zayn, Charlie and the rest of his mates walk along behind him.

'What you got there, Romelle?' asks Chris, looking at Cameron's trainers, 'Seriously? Is that Poundland's *face*?' He shakes his head. 'Now I really *have* seen it all.'

Cameron looks down at the floor, all light extinguished from his eyes. Chris and that lot rip it out of me because I'm poor, but he does the same to Cameron because he's smart. Well, not *just* because he's smart – because he's smart and kind and gentle, and he doesn't seem to understand that *sometimes* bad things happen to good people for no reason. He's also got a bit of a lisp, which he's self-conscious about, and, to be honest, that's pretty much the gift that keeps on giving to someone like Chris.

'Go on then, let me have a look at your *trainerth*,' Chris mimics.

His mates all laugh again.

'Yeah, they're thuper nice!' adds Zayn, who's basically Chris's right-hand idiot. 'Tho thmart!'

'Give it a rest,' I say, trying to sound firm, but my voice is wobbling all over the place. 'Haven't you got anything better to do?'

'*Nope,*' replies Chris, barely looking at me. 'What are they anyway? *Nikes,* right?' He shoves past me and grabs one of Cameron's trainers, holding it up to his eye, so that everyone around can see. A crowd has gathered. Chris always does his best work in front of an audience.

'*Hideous!*' he spits eventually. 'Totally overdone . . .' He peers closer at Cameron's new trainers. '*Mummy and Daddy* must have more money than sense!'

Chris glances down at my feet, a sneer curling on his lips. 'I mean, in a weird way it makes sense . . . You've got one kid with the cheapest shoes in school and then another with the most expensive – but they're both crap. Look at them, they make a great *pair!*'

He puts a hard emphasis on the word *pair,* as though

it's the cleverest pun ever. Which it clearly *isn't*, but, even so, in that moment my mind is white with anger and I can't think of a comeback.

I mean, *later* I'll come up with all sorts of clever replies that will totally cut him down to size and then the imaginary Chris in my head will run away crying while everyone hails me a hero, but for now I just clench my jaw and shake my head, a tiny jagged motion, then I look away while everyone laughs.

Well, not quite everyone.

'It's *SO* obvious you're just jealous!' rings out a voice, cutting the laughter dead. A clear solid voice that doesn't waver at all. Exactly the kind of voice that I wish I had when I was talking to Chris Tucker.

'Get lost, Kalia,' shoots Chris, eyebrows darting together in a scowl. 'None of your business, is it?'

'*Nope*,' agrees Kalia, a girl from Chris's year. Striding over, she stands directly in front of him. 'None at all. Just like it's none of yours. Unless I'm wrong and you've suddenly become *besties* with these two?'

'As if!' mutters Chris. 'Who'd want to hang round with these losers?'

Zayn coughs out a laugh.

'In *that* case . . .' continues Kalia, somehow radiating invisible waves of *DANGER*, even though she's just standing casually and her voice is no louder than usual, 'why don't you just leave them alone, and trot off to class then?'

There's a pause. Chris's friends look at each other, then glance over at Chris. Kalia smiles.

'Trot off?' says Chris. He blinks, searching desperately for a way in, a chink in Kalia's armour. 'What do you think we are, *horses*?'

A light snorting of laughter follows but clearly no one's really convinced.

'Mm-hmm,' replies Kalia, feigning confusion. 'Okaaaay . . . So, anyway, this has been *lovely* . . .' She slowly starts waving one hand and smiling in an impossibly fake way. '*Byeee*, Chris.'

'Come on, mate,' mutters Zayn, 'it's Science now. Atherton's gonna *lose it* if we're late again.'

Chris nods. Ignoring Kalia, he throws the trainer back at Cameron, hard. It smacks him on the side of the head, making him gasp and scramble about as he tries to catch it before it hits the floor.

My heart's pounding in my chest, right up into my throat – hard, heavy strokes of adrenaline. But this is different to the usual fear and shame; this is something else. That was *amazing*! I've *literally* never seen anything like it. It's like Kalia wasn't scared at *all*. Like she *genuinely* couldn't care less about what Chris *or anyone else* thought of her.

I shake my head and turn round to say something to her but she's gone, striding away on her own through the dispersing crowd.

Okaaay...
So, anyway,
this has been
LOVELY...

CHAPTER FOUR

AFTER A FEW HOURS OF SITTING, working, thinking, writing, running about a bit, and getting told off in Maths for not having my protractor, it's the end of the day and Cameron and I are finally on the way back to his.

So, let's just get this straight . . . Cameron's house is kind of unbelievable, but the most unbelievable bit about it is how neither him nor his folks seem to even notice. I mean, they've even got different fridges; there's one that's *just* for drinks – smoothies, milkshakes, flavoured water, fizzy drinks, iced tea, *whatever*! Now, I'm not saying that they've got a robot butler who makes sure that the kitchen's spotless and the cupboards are always totally full, but I *will* say that I've never seen an empty cupboard there, so you can draw your own conclusions.

Cameron opens their front door, a huge old wooden door that must weigh a ton but swings easily on well-polished thick brass hinges. Geometric tiles that are probably hundreds of years old spread across the floor, making a hypnotic pattern that leads you down the length of the hallway, which is easily as big as my living room. We take our shoes off as we walk in and I grin, like I always do – the floor's warm, *properly* warm – underfloor heating the whole way through.

'Come on, let's get a drink,' says Cameron, heading for the kitchen. 'Fizzy apple, yeah?' He runs forward, then skids across the tiles and slides on to the smooth wooden floor of the kitchen.

Turning to face me when he's come to a standstill,

Cameron looks back, one eyebrow raised. 'You coming, or what?'

I shuffle my feet; one sock's properly wet from that stupid hole in my shoe and I'm leaving soggy little prints behind me with each step.

'What's the matter?' pushes Cameron, who hasn't noticed my wet prints. 'You think you're too grown up for this now? Come on, Mr Serious, let's see what you're made of! Unless you're scared you might slip over!'

This is what's so great about Cameron: he just wants to learn stuff, make things, listen to music and have a laugh. None of the other stuff matters. With him you don't need to be cool or popular or *anything* really. In Cameron's little bubble you can just have fun – you can just *be*. We've been skidding across his floor together since I first visited his house. As I watch him turn and skid back towards me now, grinning his face almost in half, it's like I can see him at *all* those different ages. Eight-year-old Cameron on his birthday party, skidding over as I walk in through the door. Five-year-old Cameron giving me tips on the best way to skid as far as possible. Nine-year-old Cameron staring at me wide-eyed and panicked when our game got out of hand, and we accidentally smashed some plates.

'Nah, mate,' I reply, 'just didn't want to have to beat you at your own game!' I sprint forward and then, leading with the driest part of my foot, the heel, I start to skid.

'A new technique?' Cameron nods approvingly. '*Niiiice.*'

I skid all the way over and end up crashing into him. He nearly falls over, so I grab his arms to keep him upright and we wobble around for a bit, laughing like idiots.

'Let's get that juice then,' he says, draping his arm across my shoulder as we walk over to the fridge. I smile as we go, my ruined shoes and my damp sock *almost* completely forgotten.

A couple of hours later and we've come up with a bunch of new levels for this game we've been building together. Now, I know you shouldn't be all y*ay me!*, but seriously it's looking good. *Really* good. Recently I've been working on a few character designs in my sketchbook, so I take them out to show Cameron.

'Mate! These are *insane!*' he says.

I smile, a swell of pride pulsing out of my chest.

As Cameron's looking through, I skip over the page that got ruined earlier, but he stops me.

'What happened to that one?'

'Ah, yeah . . . I spilt my drink on it.'

'Right,' he says slowly. He picks up a piece of wet grass that had been trapped between the pages and inspects the streaks of mud on the page. 'What were you drinking? A grass and mud smoothie?' He smiles but not in a mean way.

So I tell him all about what happened with Chris *stupid* Tucker earlier that morning. Cameron sucks in through his teeth.

'Man, I hate that kid. You don't need a crystal ball to know his future's not looking great.'

I shrug. 'Perhaps not, but I'm not fussed about his *future*. It's the present day, where he pretty much rules the school, that bothers me!'

'I hear you.' Cameron nods his head, then he grins. 'Tell you what, though, did you see his face when Kalia squared up to him? Pretty mad, right?'

'Yeah . . . that was something else,' I say, nodding.

To be honest, I've not been able to get that moment out of my mind. I keep seeing Kalia's cool eyes holding Chris's gaze until he looked away. She looked so calm, so *strong*. I think she's pretty much the coolest person I've ever seen in real life.

'You all right, mate?' asks Cameron, lounging back in his gaming chair, peering over at me quizzically. 'You've gone all quiet.'

'Yeah. Yeah, I'm good,' I say.

Cameron looks at me. 'Look, Will . . . Chris Tucker's not going to be a problem our *whole* lives,' he says. 'I promise! Give it a few years and we'll be well out of here! You know, you'll be doing concept art or game design or something like that, and Chris Tucker'll still just be knocking around here, doing the same old, same old.'

I grin at him. 'Yeah, cheers, mate. Then we'll set up our own games company together, right?'

Cameron grins back. 'Yeah, for sure. W/C Games till I die!'

I laugh. We first decided we were going to set up a gaming company a few years ago, and for the name we just took the initials from Will and Cameron and put them together – W/C Games. I even designed the logo, until Cameron's dad pointed out that a WC is another name for a toilet. It's been a running joke ever since.

Anyway, we often chat about setting up a games company together when we're older and on a good day I still feel like it's all totally doable. But the thing is, I have lots of days that aren't *good days* – days when the rose-tinted glasses are all smudged and grimy, and other days when they're totally smashed. Still, W/C Games, it's a

nice idea – even if it's never going to be anything more than that.

'Hey, mate, look, I was

thinking –' Cameron pauses, like he's trying to pick his words carefully, like this is a bit of a speech he's been rehearsing – 'now that I've got those new trainers, I was thinking you could have my old ones, if you like? Those black ones? The Pumas? See, they're quite a narrow fit and my feet are pretty much square!' He laughs but it feels all wrong, like he's trying to make a guitar sound like a trumpet. 'See, they've always pinched a bit on the side, and I know your shoes have pretty much had it, right?'

I look at him. 'Yeah, they've had it,' I say, breathing deeply through my nose. 'But *seriously*, Cameron, I'm not looking for your hand-me-downs.'

'*Mate!* Come off it!' says Cameron, doing that horrible awkward laugh again. 'I just know that your feet are narrower than mine, so I thought you might like them. No worries, though – I can just take them to the charity shop.'

'Yeah, that'd be right . . .' I say, a bitter heat rushing through me. 'A *charity* shop? That's what I mean. I'm not

45

a *charity*! Come on, Cameron! How do you think that makes me feel?'

'I dunno!' replies Cameron, his voice rising to match mine. '*Maybe* just like I've asked if you wanted a pair of my shoes? Where's the harm in that? Man . . . you can have a real chip on your shoulder sometimes!'

'Are you for real?' I say. 'Did you *seriously* just say that?'

The world feels like it's spinning off its axis. Everything is a few degrees out of alignment.

Cameron holds his hands up. 'Look, I just think you're overreacting a bit,' he says, trying to calm things down – but I don't feel anywhere *near* ready for that.

'Overreacting?' I explode. 'Well, yeah, I guess you might think that. See, everything just *works* for you. You've got your nice house, your nice family, your nice future all lined up and ready to go. But I don't have that!' I'm shouting now. 'I don't have ANY of that! I've got nothing! No second chances. I don't even know if I've got a *first* chance! Mate, when was the last time you came for dinner at mine?'

Cameron shrugs. 'Dunno.'

'Yeah, because I *never* invite you now. Because there wouldn't be enough to eat! Because it would be cold. Because your bedroom is nearly as big as our whole flat. Don't you get it? Don't you hear what I'm saying?'

'Look, I know that things are tough right now,' says Cameron, his voice small in the huge gap that's opened up between us. 'That's why I wanted to help.'

'But this *doesn't* help!' I yell, tears blurring my vision. 'This makes me feel *worse*!'

'I just thought you might be grateful for—'

'Friends aren't *meant* to be *grateful*,' I interrupt,

Friends aren't <u>meant</u> to be grateful.

spitting the words out like poison. 'They're just meant to be *friends*!'

'Are you two okay in here?' asks Cameron's mum, poking her head round the door.

'Yeah, fine,' I say through clenched teeth, eyes prickling with a burning heat. 'I've got to go.'

'What about dinner?' she asks as I rush past her and down the stairs.

'Sorry . . .' I mutter, slipping my feet into my ruined shoes, not bothering to tie the laces.

'*Will!*' shouts Cameron behind me, as I shove open the door. 'Will, come back! Look, I'm sorry, okay?'

But I ignore him, slam the door shut behind me and run into the twilight.

CHAPTER FIVE

IT DOESN'T TAKE LONG TO LEAVE
Cameron's world and get back to reality.

Here's the thing. You can be on the smartest, *nicest*
street ever and you only need to take a handful of
turnings and you'll see a whole other side to life. We're
all tucked up, right next to each other, and that's *almost*
the problem. I mean, if you didn't know what you were
missing out on, you wouldn't miss it. Right?

Not that I'm really thinking about any of that.
My vision's blurred with tears. My feet are working

automatically, like I'm just some robot, following a hard-wired system back to where I belong – a place where half the street lights are broken and a good few windows too.

I walk through the underpass, trying to ignore the graffiti that screams from the walls, trying to ignore the dark brown stain spread across the floor where the police tape was last week, trying to ignore the buzz and flicker of the few remaining lights and the grimy cardboard lining the walls, which is going to double up as someone's bed for the night later on. Then I'm out on to the quad in the centre of Cherry Orchards where a gentle tide of litter washes across the concrete. I wade through the crisp packets and drinks cans, then I'm into the stairwell, breathing through my mouth to avoid the *very* particular fragrance – Stairwell by Calvin Klein, a scent for NOBODY. Still, it smells better than the lift, which is broken anyway. Then it's all the way up to the fourth floor and along to number 419.

Home sweet home.

I turn the key and kick the bottom of the door where

it catches. Throwing my bag off my shoulder I kick my shoes off, wriggle out of my soggy jacket and slam the door shut, using the short sharp sound to mask the swear word I hiss out.

Or at least I *thought* I'd masked the sound of it.

'Come on, Will!' comes Dad's voice from the living room. 'It can't be as bad as all *that*.'

I shake my head. It can.

It *is*.

'How come you're back so soon? I thought I was going to come and meet you at Cameron's?'

'Yeah, I came home early,' I mutter. 'I'm going to go my room, all right?'

'Whoa there!' says Dad.

I hear a grunt of exertion. I can't see into the living room as the door's shut, but I know what he's doing. He's leaning to one side, heaving himself up on the sofa arm so he can shuffle through to see me. I know how tough it is for him to move about right now, so I call out, 'Don't worry, Dad. I'll come through.'

I shoot a glance in the mirror by the door. Red eyes burning out of a pale narrow face. Dark wet hair stuck down on my forehead, neither long enough to be cool or short enough to be slick. Basically I'm a mess, and I *definitely* look like I've been crying, which is going to mean *a conversation* unless I can buy myself some time.

'Fancy a cup of tea?' I ask, turning into the kitchen and switching the kettle on. I don't need to wait for his response; he *always* fancies a cup of tea.

'Oooh yeah!' he says. 'White with twelve sugars please.'

That's just his joke. We don't have any sugar and he knows it, although we do have some powdered milk. I take my time getting the cups out, making out like I need to wash one up, but I splash my face with the water instead. Hopefully I'll look a bit less deathly now. The kettle boils and I make the teas, then I wait a bit longer, until he shouts through again, asking if I've fallen down the sink.

Taking a deep breath, I pick up the teas, push away as much of the bad feeling as possible and walk into the living room, trying my best to smile.

That was my mistake.

'Good lord, Will!' exclaims Dad, backing away in mock horror. 'What are you doing with your *face*?'

I can't help it and I smile now properly. I've never been very good at smiling on cue. Dad calls it my *photo smile* and says it's one of the more terrifying things he's ever seen.

'That's better!' he says, pale eyes scanning over me. 'So what's going on?'

'Ah, you know . . . the usual,' I say, shrugging.

'Right . . .' he says, nodding slowly, '*the usual*. Descriptive as ever! So it's the *usual* that led you to utter that *filthy* expletive as you came through the door?'

That's Dad all over. He likes words. Lots of them. The more interesting the better. Why use one when twelve will do?

'Yeah, sorry about that . . .' I mutter. I know Dad doesn't like hearing me swear. Usually I'm more careful.

'It's not the *swearing* I'm bothered about,' he says, frowning slightly. 'It's why you felt the need for it.' He looks me in the eyes. 'So *what's going on?*'

My mind whirrs. I need to think of something that *sounds* plausible, something that'll get him off my back, but that *isn't* what's really bothering me. Now, as a rule, I don't like lying to my dad, you know? We're a team. But what choice do I have? There's nothing he can do to change anything and if I tell him what's *actually* eating away at me, it'll just eat away at him too, and where's the good in that? He's in enough of a state as it is.

See, Dad's not had it easy these last few years. Mainly because he doesn't have his old job. It was just one of those things, he said at the time. They were downsizing his department at the local college. He'd been one of the technicians there for, well, for *ever*. At first, he was all positive, saying lots of things like, *You know what? I think that this could be really good for us. I'll be able to get myself a job that I really want. Make a new start!* But that was two years ago now. Cut to the present day and he feels lucky if he gets asked to fix Mrs Robinson's toilet. I guess that's a good example of *adjusting your life goals and priorities*, like they're always encouraging us to do at school.

See, the thing is, life doesn't always play along with all your grand plans. Things had been a bit tight last year when Dad got a few weeks' work on this building site where they weren't exactly *all over it* with health and safety. To be honest, I doubt they'd even *heard* of health and safety – it was properly dodgy.

A section of scaffolding came down while Dad was

walking along it and he ended up slipping down two storeys. He broke his femur, twisted his knee and tore a whole bunch of ligaments. The *best* bit is that it was all cash in hand, so there's been no sick pay, no insurance payout – no *nothing*. He can't even track down the person who hired him in the first place. It was all *a mate of a mate's got some work*.

So, yeah. He can't drive at the moment because of his leg, can't really walk much, to tell the truth, certainly can't carry anything heavy, so it's hard for him to get any work. And it's not like he was Mr Universe before, but he was *definitely* in shape, you know – *capable*. Now he's gone from looking like he could vault a six-foot wall to not being able to walk six feet without it hurting. In short, he doesn't need to hear me moan on about us being broke. He's on benefits and half our groceries come from the food bank – it's not like he doesn't know.

So I just take a deep breath and I lie.

'It's just this lad at school, who's being a bit of a tool. You know? Keeps on ripping it out of Cameron – it's getting him down a bit. He said he just wanted a bit of space.'

Dad nods, rubbing at the salt and pepper stubble on his too-thin face. 'That's rough,' he says. 'Cameron's a good kid.'

I nod but don't say anything.

'Do you want me to have a word with school?' asks Dad.

'No!' I reply too forcefully, too loud. I take a breath and run my hand back through my hair. 'No. You know how it is – these things blow over eventually.'

'All the same, a quiet word can help, and, you never know, this kid might be being a pain to other kids too. Do you know who it is?'

I shake my head. 'Cameron didn't say,' I lie as casually as I can, *worryingly* casually, in fact. I never used to be very good at lying, but I guess it's like anything – the more you do it, the better you get.

'Just someone in one of the older years,' I continue. 'Look, I'll keep an eye on it, and if it *keeps* happening, I'll let you know.'

Dad nods, then looks me right in the eye. 'And you're *sure* that's all it is?'

'Of course!'

Dad looks at me a moment longer, his blue eyes probing me, the pale irises looking greyer than they used to. He sighs and nods again. 'You're a good friend to him, Will.'

I look away, unable to hear that right now.

'So have you eaten?' asks Dad, his tone not quite disguising the fact that he *clearly* hopes that I have.

'Yeah, you know Cameron's dad!' I lie again. 'Smoked sausages, mash and *all* the veg you could imagine. Fair play, it was amazing!'

'I'll bet,' says Dad. 'Well, that's *splendid*, otherwise we'd have to go MAD tonight and crack open *another* tin of soup, right?'

'Steady on! You don't want to get *too* extravagant!'

He catches my eye and nods slightly, his eyes shining. I look away again, unable to bear his expression.

'You know what, Will?' says Dad, his voice stretching both high and low at the same time. 'It won't be like this for ever. I'll get back on my feet . . .' He looks down at his leg and grins at me. 'You know, *literally*. It'll all be good then. I *swear* it will. I just need a chance, then there'll be no looking back.' His voice wavers, then breaks, shattered by the effort at optimism. 'I'm sorry. You know that, don't you? I'm sorry things are like this.'

I grit my teeth and look down at my feet. I'm not going to cry – *no way*. 'You've nothing to be sorry for,' I reply. 'It's not like you planned it this way! It's just life, right? Besides, who needs loads of money, right? There's only so many exotic holidays we could take before we got bored of sitting around on the beach!'

He laughs, a hollow sound that echoes round the bare room. 'Yes, but . . . you go without *so* much—'

'Doesn't matter!' I interrupt. 'You're my dad! You've *always* looked out for me, and you give me *way* more than anyone could get with just *money*!'

Dad blinks quickly and now *he* looks away, running a finger under one eye. 'Thanks, Will . . .' he mutters, his voice thick and heavy.

I walk over and pat him on the shoulder. 'No worries,' I reply. 'Look, it'll get better. I *know* it will. You've got to just keep going, *right*? Like you always tell me? Just keep on trying. Things'll come good in the end.'

'Yeah . . . course they will,' he says, nodding his head and rubbing the heel of his palm into his eyes, hard. Then he looks back up at me. 'So anyway, you fancy losing at chess again?'

My eyebrows shoot upwards. 'Are you *joking*? I've won like ninety per cent of the games we've played recently.'

He shrugs. 'Yeah. *Still* . . . that means I've won ten per cent of them and *today* I'm feeling lucky! So go on then –' he nods over to the chess set by the TV – 'get it all set up!'

I get the pieces out and place them on the board. 'Black or white?' I ask. 'Not that it matters – seeing as I'm winning either way.'

'We'll see about *that*!' he says, grinning. 'Now, come on! Stop delaying the inevitable and get that board set up!'

If it wasn't me that he was talking to, and if I didn't know just how broken he was, that smile would *almost* be convincing.

CHAPTER SIX

JOLTING AWAKE, I'M PULLED OUT of whatever dream I was in.

My heart's pounding and despite the chill of the night, my thin duvet's damp with sweat. Dad's asleep in the room next to mine. I can hear him breathing – slow and steady, in and out. *Seriously*, the walls in here are like paper.

I roll over and close my eyes, trying to calm my breathing, calm my

mind. But it's no good. I just can't sleep. My brain's buzzing and sparking like raw electricity – wild, directionless and angry. After what feels like hours of lying there, I get up. But *now* what? Our tiny flat presses in at me with cold calloused hands. I could put the TV on, watch a DVD or something, but I don't want to wake Dad. So I find myself

a jacket, then I'm slipping out of the
door and away.

Now, I know it's not a great idea
to go for a stroll round here
at whatever o'clock in the
morning it is, but *honestly*
the thought of sitting

around in our flat is more than I can bear right now. At least out here there's a bit more space, the illusion of freedom. Besides, I can avoid all the places I know are *properly* dodgy.

A cool wind pushes me down the empty streets that seem cleaner and clearer now, without the harsh unflinching daylight revealing all their dirty secrets. Everything is quiet and still, as though I'm the only person alive, like this is *my* world, and it's all just for me. I don't see anyone, any *sign* of anyone. No cars streak past, filling the night with thudding music. There are no angry shouts ringing out of other people's flats, no sirens, no distant shattering glass, no wild laughter, no screaming or running feet.

Just stillness.

Street lights gleam as the buildings reach up into the cool night sky and for the first time in ages I feel a sense of peace.

The next moment, a piercing sound rings out just by my ear. I spin round, heart racing as a gust of wind beats past me. Something huge shoots past and *whooshes* overhead. The air swirls and eddies in its wake, filled with a scent that I can't place – fresh, wild and free. Something drifts down from the sky – small, pale, almost silver. It *can't* be snow, can it? I mean, sure, it's cold but it's *way* too early for that, isn't it?

I reach my hand up and realise that it's a feather. A soft downy feather. It seems to glow in my hand beneath the street light. So perfect. So improbable.

The call rings out again. A piercing screech. I spin round. Perching on a graffiti-covered postbox is a massive silver bird. Sharp talons grip the painted iron as it regards me with pale round eyes over a smooth curved beak that ends in a point so fine it could have been carved with a diamond.

Without taking its eyes off me the bird stretches lazily, opening its wings wider than I'm tall, maybe even wider than *Dad's* tall – and he's nearly six foot. Tilting its head to one side and then the other, the bird tucks itself neatly back up and perches there, calmly regarding me.

I've never seen an owl before. At least not in real life, so I had no idea they were quite so . . . *massive*. And perhaps they aren't usually . . . but *this* one is. I stand there, frozen. Unable to move, think or do *anything* really. I'm just swept up into the gravitational pull of this creature in front of me.

Now, ordinarily if I were faced with a wild animal with a wingspan like that, talons as long as my fingers and a beak that's *literally* designed for tearing flesh, I might be at least a *bit* scared, or to be more honest completely terrified, but I don't feel *any* of that. For some reason I just feel this sense of intense calm wash over me as the owl stares at me, unblinking, with its huge round eyes gleaming with a soft reflective light like mercury.

I've no idea how long I'm standing there, but all of a sudden I realise that no one would *ever* believe this. I need proof. You know? *Pictures or it didn't happen* . . . I fumble around in my pocket, grabbing for my phone and shoot a glance down, selecting the camera. As I do that, a sudden *whoosh* cuts through the air and a gust of wind almost throws me off balance.

When I look back, the owl is gone.

You might think I'd feel disappointed, or upset that I didn't get a photo, but actually *no*. I don't feel that at all. After all, I still have the silver feather clamped between my fingers *and* I've got the memory of the owl. Its complete physical *presence* is burned into my mind with more depth than any photograph could hope to compete with.

Besides, I suddenly realise that I don't even *want* to tell anyone about the owl – about this moment – it's all mine. Something just for me.

CHAPTER SEVEN

LUCKILY DAD WAS STILL ASLEEP
when I got in. Pushing our front door open as quietly as
I could, I realised he'd have lost his mind if he'd woken
up and found that I was just *not there*.

There's NO WAY he'd let me go out wandering around
at that time of night, but, still, he *didn't* know, and I
wasn't about to tell him. So . . . no harm done.

I climb back into bed, suddenly feeling tired, but not
the scratchy, wired exhaustion I'm used to – this was a
deep cleansing feeling of calm. Like lowering yourself

into a warm bath. I close my eyes and settle back into the pillows, and then at some point I guess I must have drifted off to sleep.

That strange sensation of calm and peace stayed with me . . . basically until I found myself back at school the next day.

You know what an argument with your best friend feels like? It's like you're wearing your shirt the wrong way round and your trousers back to front. Everything would look pretty much the same from a distance, but up close it's all kinds of wrong.

I was a bit late in, and when I get into History Cameron's moved seats and is now sitting next to Elsie Woodleigh, even though I know *full well* that she winds him up because she's always chatting and never pays any attention in lessons. If there's one thing that Cameron is, it's focused. I genuinely can't believe that despite *everything* he'd rather sit next to her than me. I guess things must be *really* bad. On the way in I'd been running through everything in my mind, working out how to smooth things over with him, but it doesn't look like *that's* happening any time soon.

'Sorry I'm late, miss,' I mutter as I shuffle in and go to take my seat, alone at the desk I usually share with Cameron.

'That's okay, Will,' says Mrs Unwin. 'I *assume* you've informed the office?'

'Yes, miss,' I reply, not adding that it was waiting for the massive queue at reception that made me twice as late as I was – some things *really* aren't worth going into.

'Very good.' Mrs Unwin nods. 'Now, Will, would you like to share your response to the homework?' She pauses and looks around the room. 'I'm *assuming* that everyone here has remembered to bring in their piece on medieval castle fortifications?'

Mrs Unwin makes a lot of assumptions.

My heart sinks even further, dropping through the wet paper bag I've been storing it in and tumbling away somewhere far beneath me. *The homework* . . . I close my eyes, willing myself to be anywhere that isn't here.

Unfortunately when I open my eyes again I'm still trapped in my History lesson, hand still gripping the back of my seat, not yet sat down and everyone looking at me.

'So what did you focus on, Will?' she asks.

My mouth fills with cotton wool and sawdust. I swallow hard. 'I . . . er, I didn't do it, miss,' I mutter.

Mrs Unwin nods and breathes heavily out through her nose. 'You *haven't* done it?'

'No, miss,' I reply. What was she was *hoping* I'd say?

Maybe something like: *Only joking! I actually DID do the homework! That's right! I crafted a handmade model of a working castle gate out of lollipop sticks, cardboard, string and glue with my dad while we were sat in our cosy living room, watching the History Channel on Sky+ for research. Then we got out all our paints and brushes and sat there painting away while we waited for our pizza delivery to arrive.*

I mean, *seriously*! How am I going to make a model out of *things that you'll just have at home* when we don't have anything at home? And, sure, I know that Mrs

Unwin said we could also have just done a poster, and, *sure*, I know she leaves a few sheets of paper and pens by the door for *anyone who might need some materials*, but I don't want to have to do that. It's like admitting defeat, you know? I guess that's how Dad feels about the food banks. I mean, I'm always saying we should go along, get a few bits, but he always seems to find some excuse not to.

'So is there any particular reason *why* you didn't do the homework?' Mrs Unwin pushes.

I shake my head. 'I just forgot, miss,' I mutter. To be honest, that was also true. I did completely forget about it.

Mrs Unwin peers over her glasses at me. 'I assume you know that means a detention, Will?'

'You *assume* correctly, miss,' I hear myself saying.

It just kind of slips out and there's this semi-audible gasp from the class. I'm not the kind of person who's rude to the teachers. I never act up or get in trouble – at least, I never used to, but all these *assumptions* are really getting on my nerves.

'Rudeness is UNACCEPTABLE, Will,' states Mrs Unwin. 'You'll be getting a negative for that.'

I shrug, even though my heart is pounding.

Mrs Unwin shakes her head and continues to stare at me with this whole *I'm-not-angry-I'm-just-disappointed* look. The rest of the class is starting to get a bit lively, so eventually she turns away and clears her throat. '*Ummmm* . . . I don't believe that I opened a discussion! Fatima, how did *you* respond to the project?'

Fatima stands up, pulling an elaborate 3D-printed drawbridge and portcullis out of her bright orange rucksack as I sit heavily down, my own scuffed, grubby three-year-old school bag falling by my feet.

The rest of school's just, you know, *schooly*, although it's this weird, alternative-reality version of school where me and Cameron don't even make eye contact let alone talk. You know I said earlier that Cameron's my best friend? I guess I should have said he's pretty much my *only* friend. So without him to talk to I'm stuck on my own. I do see Kalia across the canteen at lunchtime, and I *think* she might have smiled at me, but it was kind of sunny so she might have just been looking in my direction and squinting. I sort of half waved and then panicked in case she *hadn't* been smiling at me at all. So I spun round, trying to look like I'd just remembered that I had something urgent to do, and walked out. I can be such an idiot sometimes . . . Seriously, who even does that kind of thing?

The *only* good thing about the day is that we have Art last thing, and getting into that room is like coming home – if, you know, your home is somewhere that you *like* being. It's the whole thing, you know? Not just the drawing and the painting; it's the whole lot. The smell of it – the paints, the clay, the white spirit – everything. It all merges together to just make me feel – I don't know – calm. It helps that Mr Prince's decent too – *properly* decent. Sometimes he plays music in the lessons and even gives me cartridge paper to take home to draw on. He's got this trick to cut the huge sheets down to

Schhhzzzzz!

size, just using a steel ruler. He folds it over, takes out his trusty measuring blade and slides it across the fold. *Schhhhzzzzzzzz* – and the paper's cut. I love it. There's no WAY I'd have that sort of paper otherwise. You know, *proper* paper – *art* paper – with an actual bite to it, paper that you can *feel* while you draw on it, not like the plastic-smooth printer paper I normally use.

I walk through the door and already I feel a little bit better.

'So how's your day going, Will?' asks Mr Prince, who's *clearly* been briefed on how my day's been going so far.

'Not so great, sir,' I mutter.

'Okay . . .' says Mr Prince evenly. 'I know how *that* feels.'

And that's it. He doesn't say anything to try to make me feel better, or find out *why* it's not been a good day, or why I acted up with Mrs Unwin, and weirdly that makes me feel a bit better.

He just claps me on the back with one of his huge hands and I go over to open my drawer and take out the still life I've been working on. To be honest, I'm not *really* into that sort of thing, drawing fruits and old kettles and stuff, or at least I wasn't until Mr Prince pointed out that if you want to draw armour you need to know how to draw shiny metal, and that an orc's skin is all soft and pitted, kind of like an old avocado. So now I can see the point in it, even if I don't enjoy it as much as I enjoy drawing from my imagination.

Mr Prince then addresses the whole class, but he makes sure that he catches my eye as he speaks. 'This afternoon I thought we might do something a bit different,' he says. 'You've all been working *really* hard on your still-life pieces, so I thought we'd take a bit of time to just have some fun. Okay? So for the rest of today I want you to draw or paint *anything* that captures your imagination. Something that feels relevant to *you*. Anything you like. Animal, vegetable, mineral, *whatever*! The only important thing is that you make the image you *want* to make, however you want to make it. All right?'

There's a buzz of excitement as we all get out fresh

sheets of paper. Alia asks if she can make a sculpture and Mr Prince grins, opening his hands wide. 'Like I said . . . whatever you want!'

For the first time today I feel excited. I could draw a cleric about to do battle with some elven renegades or a dragon obliterating a whole village, a whole citadel, the whole *world*! But as I sit there, staring at the paper in

front of me, there's only one image in my mind . . .

Ordinarily I draw pretty tight. You know? I like to use hard pencils and draw everything kind of small and super detailed. But for some reason I find myself reaching for the biggest paintbrush I can find. I mix up a diluted blue wash. Then I feel my way over the whole sheet of paper, roughly indicating the basic form of the owl. I don't even have any reference. I don't need it. Seriously, that owl is

locked in my mind.

As I'm sliding the brush around, I feel like I can see the curved blade of the beak on the paper even before I've painted it. The feathers on the wings just appear before me as the watery paint swirls and bleeds across the image, but that doesn't spoil the painting – if anything, it adds to it. Having finished with the pale blues, I mix up a thicker night-sky shade that's almost black. Hard crevices of shadow are carved in, as the image becomes clearer and stronger but still just as loose. Just as free. After that, it's a few highlights, the gleam of the eyes, the silver wingtips, the suggestion of stars in the background, and then, *boom!* Less than forty-five minutes later, it's finished.

I put down the paintbrush and stand back from the table, feeling strangely dizzy – my heart and mind are racing as I look at the best thing that I've *ever* done. Perhaps even the best thing I'll *ever* do.

I didn't realise that Mr Prince had been standing behind me until he gently clears his throat. Usually I hate it when someone watches me drawing, but today it didn't matter at all. Although, to be honest, it didn't really feel like I was the one doing the work. It's weird, it was more like the image was just *happening* and all I did was move the brush around – if that makes any sense at all?

'That's incredible,' says Mr Prince. 'Really, it's *remarkable* . . .' His warm deep voice pauses, and he shakes his head, almost laughing.

'Thanks, sir,' I reply.

Usually I'm about as happy to get a compliment as a cat is to be sprayed with cold water, but on this occasion I smile. He's right. It really is something special – even *I* can see that.

'No elves today?' he adds, digging me lightly on the arm with his elbow.

'Not today, sir,' I reply.

'So what inspired this, Will?' he asks, kind of confused but also pleased, perhaps even proud.

'Well . . .' I begin slowly. Mr Prince is nice and all, but, even so, that moment last night is *mine*, and I don't really feel like talking about it. 'They're just cool, aren't they?

Owls, I mean.'

'They certainly are,' he says, shaking his head slowly. 'You know? That's what I love about this job. There's always a surprise, every single day. Some surprises are . . . *less* welcome, but this –' he glances at me, eyes shining before he looks back at my painting – 'this painting *speaks* to me. It really *says* something. And I'll be honest with you, Will, that's rare . . .' He looks at me again. 'I'm sure I don't need to tell you, Will, but that's art.' His eyes are glued to the painting. 'What you've done right there, that's *real* art.'

And you know what? I think he might be right.

He pauses again and we both look back at the painting in silence. I see the owl as I saw her last night, a lonely figure, silver wings stretched wide, gleaming bright, shining in an oppressive darkness. Soaring past me to an unknown place, full of freedom, strength and a pure burning wildness.

CHAPTER EIGHT

MR PRINCE HOLDS UP MY PAINTING and everyone makes a really big deal out of it. Even Omari, who usually has some sort of diss for whatever I've done, admits that it's pretty good, although he looks like he's chewing wasps at the same time.

Still, it feels good, you know? Properly good. There's a bunch of kids in there and suddenly they're all looking at me like someone who can actually *DO* something, not just some weirdo with the wrong shoes and a rubbish coat.

But then the lesson's over. Even as I'm walking out of

the door, that warm, calm feeling fades. Everyone else is going home, laughing and joking in twos or threes while I skulk off on my own to sign in for detention.

And who do you think is sat in there on detention duty, waiting for me? Mrs Unwin.

The lecture goes pretty much how you'd expect. I've heard it all before, after all.

Do I know why I'm here? *Yes.*

Do I understand how important it is for there to be mutual respect between teachers and students? *Yes.*

Do I regret my choice of actions and would I do things differently if given another opportunity? *Yes.*

The trouble is that it's very easy to say *yes* but to secretly think *no* or more to the point *whatever*, so it's just this weird little dance that we're doing right now. Still, I say what needs to be said, hoping that it'll speed things along a bit, and you know what? It seems like it does.

I get handed my assignment sheet and read through it. *Simple* – downloading the music for Monday's assembly down in the ITC suite. I start to leave when Mrs Unwin puts her hand out, gently blocking my path.

'Hang on a minute, Will,' she says. 'Look, I *know* you're a good kid. And I *know* that what happened today is out of character, so I'm not going to note it down on your personal record *or* send it home. Okay?'

I nod and a slight weight lifts off me. 'Thanks, miss,' I say, making sure that I look her in the eye while I'm speaking – teachers are big on that. And, to be fair, that's decent of her – I *really* didn't want to have to explain any of this to Dad, and now he'll never need to know.

'Look, Will, is everything okay? You know, at home, any problems?'

Now, I appreciate the sentiment, I really do, but there's no WAY I'm telling her *anything*! Firstly, I just don't feel like it, and secondly, I dunno . . . it just feels a bit, you know, disloyal. Like I'd be letting Dad down by telling her what life at home's *actually* like. So instead I put on my best breezy face and even sort of sheepishly smile. 'Yeah, all good, thanks, miss. I just didn't sleep very well last night and kind of woke up on the wrong side of bed, you know?'

'I know that one,' she says with a smile. 'Well, make sure you try to get enough sleep, okay? It is *very* important.'

'Will do,' I reply. I think I might even have saluted. She smiles at me then says, 'I *assume* you understand the task you've been assigned?'

I guess pretty much everything that Mrs Unwin says is an assumption of some kind, but since flagging that up is what got me into trouble in the first place I do *everything* I can to let that most recent one just wash right past.

'Yes, miss,' I reply, smiling. 'Downloading the music for Monday's assembly – shouldn't take me too long.'

She smiles at me. 'Well, good luck with it, Will. And you have a nice weekend.'

'Thanks, miss. You too,' I reply, then I'm off to the ITC suite.

Finding the song's easy. I knew it would be. They wanted this piece called 'Habanera' by some old dead dude called Bizet. I'd have been done in about five minutes, but there are loads of versions of the song and I can't work out which one I like the best, so I spend about half an hour listening to them all until I find one that I *really* like. Tell you what, it's a pretty sweet piece actually. If you put a beat over it, I reckon you'd have a hit on your hands. Then I rip the audio from a YouTube video and drop it in to the PowerPoint.

And then that's it – my work here is *done*. Putting down the name of the song in the Notes app on my phone, I shoulder my bag and push open the door of the ITC suite. By this point I'm feeling *properly* hungry, so I head over to where the school buses come in. I know that seems like a random thing to do, but there's this bar there to stop everyone running straight into the road and getting mowed down by the traffic. While the kids are waiting for their buses, they spin round over it, and when they do it's like they're small-change Catherine wheels, shooting coins out of their pockets like sparks. Most people think it's grotty to bother looking around for any money that they've dropped, so they just leave it. I think it's stupid *not* to . . . Anyway, their loss, my gain. I found a two-pound coin there the other day. So who's laughing now?

Well, not me as it turns out.

I spent nearly ten minutes searching, but all I pick up is thirty-five pence. To tell the truth, I'm a bit gutted. I was hoping I'd find enough to get chips on the walk home – still, it's thirty-five pence more than I had earlier, so I guess I should take that as a win.

Since I'm not heading towards the chippy, there's no need to go past the high street, so I take another route. It's not until I'm almost there that I'm walking directly towards the spot where I saw the owl last night.

So now my chest is tight, and I've got this weird thrumming sensation in my stomach. It's a bit like when I was little and Dad took me to the swimming pool with all the big slides for the first time. You know . . . excited but nervous too.

I mean, deep down, I *know* it's stupid. What are the chances of having a once-in-a-lifetime encounter two days in a row? The clue's in the name . . . It's not very likely at all. All the same, it still surprises me how I feel when I turn the corner.

And there it is . . .

Nothing.

Just a battered old postbox covered in old stickers and spray paint, standing on a dirty street corner where nobody would *usually* be unless they were going somewhere else.

Even though I *knew* it was impossible, even though I *knew* it was stupid, I'd still hoped that I *might* find the owl there again. But of course I didn't. That's just not how life works, is it? I shoulder my bag and walk on through the darkening evening.

It's a dangerous thing, hope.

CHAPTER NINE

I HAD THIS THING I USED TO DO a couple of years back where I kept a chart of my days on a sheet of graph paper. You know, ranking them by colour, so the square for a good day was coloured in *green*, *orange* was okay and *red* was BAD.

I stopped after a while. Firstly, it just got depressing, but *also* it's hard to make the call. Most of my actual *days* are red, but there are moments that are *definitely* green – you know, like the owl, my painting. I guess the trick is to hang on to all the green *moments* as they

94

happen, before they get lost in a sea of red?

'You all right, Will?' calls Dad as I walk into our flat. I sniff. It smells different to usual. What *is* it? It's not fried onions, is it? Dad's not *actually* cooking, is he?

'I made a stew,' calls Dad from the kitchen. 'Something to fuel you up for the bus ride to Mum's later. I know you hate the bus.'

'You made *stew*? What happened? You catch a squirrel out in the quad or something?'

Dad laughs and it's a *real* laugh. 'No, not yet – they're still too quick for me.'

'Seriously, though,' I press. 'Where d'you get the money?'

'Well, it was one of those cheap bruised veg boxes at Aldi and, to be fair, the meat's just a pack of sausages, so I guess that makes it a more of a casserole?'

'All the same . . .' I look over at the pan. 'You've actually got the hob on!'

'Look, I don't want to count any chickens . . .' says Dad, and my heart sinks. My dad is an *expert* chicken counter. I know full well that he's already numbered every single one of those theoretical hens and is right now buying seed for the massive chicken farm that he's built in his head.

He grins as he catches my eye. 'The thing is . . . I had an interview today and it went well. *Really* well. I don't need a driving licence. It's mainly desk work, and the building's got a lift so I won't slow everyone down going up the steps.' His face is all shining now, and I don't want to be the one to tell him that he's talking like he's *already* been offered the job.

'Plus, I got a *really* good feeling from the lady doing the interview, you know. She was nice. She even said, "See you soon."'

My heart sinks further. Seriously, it's like he's *my* kid and I need to tell him that the tooth fairy might not *actually* be real. I take a deep breath. 'I mean . . . that's great and all. But it's not a done deal, is it? We still need to pay for my bus ride tonight *and* next week's food as well.'

Dad waves his hand dismissively. 'It's fine. I got a bit of cash from Damien to see us through.'

'Are you *joking*?'

My jaw *literally* drops, hanging open like a trapdoor. Damien's the local loan shark and just about as hard as they come.

'*Damien?* Are we talking about the same Damien? Damien Forsyth? Have you heard what happens to people that don't pay him back on time?'

'Look, I'm sure he's not as bad as all that,' says Dad. 'It's probably just exaggerated. You know, to make sure people don't default on their loans.'

'*Default on their loans?*' My voice is rising almost to a shout. 'He's not a *building society*!' I shake my head. 'And you're happy to test that theory, are you? What if you don't get this job? What if you *can't* pay him back?' My heart's pounding like I've just done that stupid beep test at school.

'Look, don't worry about it,' says Dad, genuinely acting like he's not got a care in the world. 'Like I say . . . I've got a good feeling about this.'

I feel like I've been carved out of ice and can hear the creaking sound of hairline fractures racing through my entire life while everything that's sensible and normal slowly collapses inwards. *Damien Forsyth?* When we first moved here, Dad specifically told me not to go near him. He said, literally, word for word: *Damien Forsyth is like a disease that infects this whole place. He preys on the weak and the vulnerable, exploiting bad luck for his own gain. Seriously, Will, just don't go near him, or anyone who associates with him.*

So I guess this means we're now officially weak, vulnerable and unlucky.

Brilliant.

All of a sudden, I can't wait to go to Mum's later on. I hadn't been that fussed about it before, but right now I'd take *anywhere* over here.

ACT
TWO

CHAPTER TEN

TELL YOU WHAT, IT IS COLD.
I don't know what's wrong with these buses. It's like
the air conditioning's only got two settings. Dry, dusty,
baking heat and face-numbingly freezing. It's a shame
they only use the hot setting in the middle of summer.

So I'm bumping along the potholed roads on the way
to Mum's, the music in my headphones just about keeping
the world at bay. Some guy on the seat in front scowls
at me, but I ignore him and turn the music up louder,
losing myself within the sound, trying to get transported

somewhere else, trying to believe that as long as the song lasts I'm not *actually* me – I'm someone else somewhere completely different.

Fifty minutes later and I get off at the closest bus stop to Mum's. She lives on the edge of this small market town where basically nothing happens – *ever*. It's kind of dull, but at least it's not our flat in Cherry Orchards.

I walk along the river for five or so minutes and then get to the road that Mum lives on. Twin rows of Victorian terraces glare at each other from either side of the narrow street, or at least they *try* to but there are cars and vans blocking the view, parked haphazardly all along the pavements. I guess these would have been nice houses once, but most of them are flats now, so it feels like *way* more people live round here than there's room for.

Standing outside the door a moment, I take a deep breath. I always find it weird coming here.

So what to say about Mum? Well, *firstly*, I love her. I mean, she's my mum, right? It's just that, you know, things *did* go downhill when she left. I know that it wasn't *because* she left. Dad always makes that *really* clear. None of this is her fault – he says that's something called a *false equivalence*. It was just a decision that they came to together – because they weren't in love any more.

And it's not like she left Dad when he lost his job or when he got injured or anything. She didn't even leave him for Greg. No, when Mum moved out Dad was still fit and healthy, still working at the college, still having a laugh and a joke. To be honest, I'm pretty much sure that she doesn't even *really* know the state that he's currently in. I mean, I've not told her, and Dad *certainly* hasn't. He's like that, my dad – doesn't want *anyone* feeling sorry for him. You know, doesn't want any pity or charity. But yeah, I find it weird coming here all the same. I think a big part of that is because Greg is *always* here.

I mean, I suppose it *is* his flat, so I guess he has a right to be there. But it doesn't mean I have to like it.

I ring the buzzer and hear Greg's voice crackle through the intercom.

'He-lllo?'

It drives nails through me. Even that. One word. *Hello*. Obviously it's not the word itself; it's the way he says it. The way that he drags it out, like it's made of chewing gum and he's seeing how far he can stretch it before it snaps. I suddenly feel like I want to scream the worst swear word I can think of at the top of my lungs, and it takes everything I've got NOT to do that.

Instead, I take a deep breath and just say, 'All right, Greg?' in what I hope is a friendly voice. 'It's me, Will. Is Mum there?' Even though I know full well that she's there. I've just had a text from her saying, *C U in 5, sweetheart X.*

'Hey, Will!' says Greg. 'Come on up, buddy!'

Buddy? Seriously? I shake my head.

The door buzzes and I push it open, walking into the communal hallway. There are bikes leaned up against the wall, bikes hanging from the ceiling and even bikes chained up on the banisters. Seriously, it looks like a bomb went off in a bike factory. I fight my way past them all and up to the second floor.

Mum's waiting for me, leaning against the door frame, smiling easily, her hair still brown, only a couple of grey hairs, hardly any wrinkles, even when she smiles, and she smiles a lot. She still looks pretty much how she did when I was little, whereas Dad looks like someone made a bad copy of the person he used to be, thinned out all his hair and added a whole load of wrinkles.

'Will!' says Mum, coming towards me with her arms wide, pulling me into a hug. 'You okay, love?' she whispers, holding me tight. Those simple words melt into me, almost deep enough to break through the shell that's formed around the person that *I* used to be. But I'm not that kid any more; I'm someone else too –

and there's nothing anyone can do to just magic things better now. So what's the point in getting into it?

'Yeah. Good, thanks,' I say, pulling out of the hug. 'How about you two?'

'Ah, you know,' says Mum, grinning over at Greg who's picked up a battered acoustic guitar, 'we're pretty much the embodiment of rock and roll.'

'Yep,' agrees Greg, wriggling his feet into some pink novelty slippers. He smiles back at my mum as he starts playing an old Oasis song on the guitar.

I roll my eyes. Greg's just so . . . *Greg*.

But Mum laughs, and when she does their living room glows – a hazy bubble of warmth and happiness that radiates out from her, and I can *see* how happy they are.

See, that's the problem. I *know* that Mum loves Greg, and that he loves her. Any idiot can see that. I also know that on paper he's *way* better for her than Dad was. They both love music and are *really* into plays, musicals, all that sort of thing. The walls of Greg's flat are lined with DVDs, CDs and old tapes that he's had since the nineties.

Dad was never really all that fussed about any of that stuff. I mean, don't get me wrong, he likes a good tune, but he was always more into reading, going to the gym, rock climbing and fixing stuff.

So, yeah, I *know* that Mum and Greg love each other, and in all seriousness that's great – Mum deserves to be happy. But I'm stood there right now all the same, slap bang in the middle of that bubble of warmth and light, and I just don't know where I'm meant to fit in with it all. You know? It's weird, it's like it's all happening *around* me, but I just don't feel it.

CHAPTER ELEVEN

I SLEEP ON A PULL-OUT FUTON in the tiny box room at Mum's where there's barely any room to even pull the bed out. It's where Greg keeps all the CDs that he can't fit in the living room and about twelve hundred different guitars. I mean, that's an exaggeration, but seriously there are *loads*.

When I wake up, I smell bacon cooking and jump out of bed. Well, I *wriggle* out of bed, trying to avoid catching myself on any of the instruments hanging on the walls, and carefully put my clothes on, but, you know, I do it quickly.

Mum's in the kitchen. It's kind of cramped and I heave myself on to the worktop in the corner so I'm out of the way.

'Morning, love!' she says, smiling. 'Sleep all right?'

'Yeah,' I reply. 'It's a good job I don't snore, though, the strings on those guitars vibrate whenever you make a sound louder than a whisper!'

'Why do you think I make Greg keep them all in there!' says Mum with a laugh. 'Fancy a bacon sarnie or is that a silly question?'

'Does a bear use the lavatorial facilities in the woods?'

Mum grins. 'I remember when your dad first said that! He's certainly got a way with words.'

'You're not wrong.'

We both smile for a while, then Mum's smile slowly fades.

'And how is he? Your dad?'

'Ah, you know . . .' I try to sound breezy. 'Same old, same old.'

Mum frowns. 'Just because Sally said something about an accident at work?'

See, *this* is the trouble with leading a double life. You've got to keep all your stories straight with *everyone*. And people like Sally, Mum's old friend who still lives a few streets away from me and Dad, don't make *that* any easier.

'Ah, right, *yeah* –' I shrug – 'that! Yeah, that was all a bit of a nightmare. He had to take a couple of weeks off, but he's loads better now.'

Mum looks at me, her eyes narrow and she chews at her bottom lip. 'So he's back at work?'

'*Yep*,' I say, super breezy, like everything's TOTALLY fine. 'Well . . . he's looking for a new one. You know Dad – not one to sit around on his backside!'

'Yes, I know your dad,' says Mum, nodding briskly, her eyes shining, 'and I know that he's proud . . .' She pauses. 'So everything's *really* okay?'

I look Mum dead in the eyes and even do a little laugh. 'Look, I'm not going to lie . . .' I say, layering up another couple of lies that are close enough to the truth to almost fool me. 'We were a bit strapped for a while, when Dad wasn't working, and, sure, all the jobs he gets at the minute are like zero-hours things with no security, so *that* gets him down a bit, but *basically* we're good.'

Like I say, Mum and Greg aren't rolling in it. They can have the heating on, and buying a pack of bacon's no huge deal, but it's not like they can *actually* help. Not *really*. So what's the point in laying it on them? Mum's working at a playgroup and Greg teaches guitar lessons and plays in some Americana pub band at the weekends, so they're hardly on the rich list. Besides, Mum *does* help when she can – passing me the odd fiver and every month she puts money into Dad's bank towards food and clothes for me, but, you know, it's never *enough*. Not when Dad's not working.

'So you don't need to worry about us!' I say, patting her on the shoulder.

Mum pulls me into a tight hug. 'But you *would* say, wouldn't you?' she whispered. 'You know, if you needed help?'

'Course I would!' I lie.

We stay there like that for a while, me hugging her until the bacon starts to smell like it's burning, then Mum spins round to pull it out from under the grill.

'Besides . . .' I add, 'Dad had an interview the other day, and he got a *really* good feeling. It's an office job, so it'll be perfect until his leg's one hundred per cent better. Now, he's not counting any chickens—'

'As *if*!' Mum interrupts, laughing, although her face looks strained. 'I do *actually* know him, remember?' She sighs. 'All the same, I hope it works out for him, Will. I really do.'

Greg leans in round the door, smiling as he *completely* murders the moment. 'Last one up, am I?' he asks, and then sniffs the air. 'Mmm, bacon! Looks like I timed it just right!'

'Well, you can wash up!' says Mum, throwing a tea towel at Greg's face.

He gasps, pretending to be outraged and then opens the cupboard by the door. The room suddenly feels *far* too small.

'Fair enough . . .' he says, pulling out two bottles and looking over at me. 'Brown sauce or red, Will?'

'Neither . . .' I reply. Then after a pause I think to add, '*Thanks.*'

Mum hands me my sandwich. The bread's fresh and warm with a crispy crust. Inside, the bacon's all layered up – there must be like five rashers or something – and it's the good stuff too, the *thick* stuff. I take a huge bite and close my eyes. All of a sudden, I'm eight years old again. Way back before Mum left – when we were all

living together in the old house, back when we'd *always* have bacon sarnies on the weekend – back when we were happy.

Well, back when I was happy.

Then Greg speaks and slowly I open my eyes – my vision splintering into tiny shards that tinkle around my feet.

'So, Will . . . your mum and I are going to head over to a guitar exhibition at the museum in town this morning. Do you fancy coming along?'

I'd rather lick my fingers and stick them in a live plug socket.

'No thanks,' I reply. 'I've got to get a haircut.'

Internally I shake my head. *Get a haircut?* Where did *that* come from?

'Okay, love,' says Mum, rooting around in her purse. 'That'll be nice; it *is* getting a bit shaggy. Do you want some cash towards it? I've got a fiver in here somewhere . . .'

She finds a five-pound note and holds it out towards me.

'Thanks, Mum!' I say, taking the note and putting it in my pocket.

'Well, if you're sure,' says Greg. 'It's all these guitars that used to be owned by famous musicians. They've even got one that Paul McCartney once played!'

'*Wow*,' I say, hoping that it doesn't sound as sarcastic as I'm feeling, 'that sounds great, but seriously, you two go along, I'll catch up with you later on.'

Then I turn my attention back to the bacon sarnie, hoping it can weave its time-travelling magic spell again – but it doesn't.

It still tastes great, though, so, you know, I'll take that.

CHAPTER TWELVE

Now, I have a bit of a problem...

I need a haircut by the time Mum and Greg get back from their exhibition. I mean, it's not the biggest problem in the world, but, still, it needs some thought. Trouble is, a haircut's pricey and even with the fiver Mum gave me, there's no way I can scrape enough together.

The idea hits me suddenly, like all the best ideas.

DIY.

I know Greg's got a beard trimmer; it's basically like a set of mini hair clippers. I can just do a number four all over and that'll be that. I mean, sure, it's not a *great* look, but, to be fair, anything's better than what I've got going on at the minute.

Reaching into the bathroom cabinet I pull out the beard trimmer. It's covered in lots of tiny bits of Greg's beard hairs, which makes me feel all kinds of gross. I brush them off as best I can, then look through the various comb guards for one that's the right length.

Now, I'll be honest, I've never cut my own hair before, but how hard can it be? I mean, it's not like I'm trying to do some tight fade or something, I'm just doing the whole lot the same length – easy.

I clip on the attachment and turn the beard trimmer on. It even sounds like the clippers at the barber's and there's a soft reassuring buzz as the trimmer vibrates slightly in my hand. Starting low, I gently slide the trimmer up the side of my head, watching as clumps of my hair drift down like confetti.

I pause and run my fingers up the side of my head. God, that feels better – so much lighter. I'm smiling now, nodding as I look at myself in the mirror – this is going to look great.

The trimmer hums back into life and I carry on, working my way round the sides and the back. I mean, sure it looks kind of funny right now, with this weird long bit on the top, but I'll sort that out afterwards.

Everything's going brilliantly, until I hear a crack and a small shard of plastic pings into the sink, followed by a larger piece of plastic as the guard falls off and then a whole *load* more hair drifts down and the trimmer gets caught in the long bit of hair on the top, chewing it up like an angry lawnmower.

Now, I don't know if you've ever used hair clippers, but they have these little metal teeth that slide across each other – they're what *actually* cuts the hair, and they cut it *short*, basically bald. It's the different combs that give you the different lengths. So, yeah, without the comb guard, I've managed to carve a totally bald strip out of my hair. Heart racing, I yank the trimmer out of my tangled hair, where it's busy hacking more weird bald patches up the side of my head. Frantically I turn it off and stand there sort of gasping, looking at the disaster in the mirror.

It's bad.

Really bad.

I've got this long bit on top that hangs down and then it's all short at the sides, apart from the chunks where it's *literally* bald.

A rush of heat pulses through me as I stare at myself in the mirror.

I look like an absolute state.

CHAPTER THIRTEEN

I'M NOT SURE HOW LONG I'M stood there, staring slack-jawed at my reflection, but after a while I pull myself together and start trying to work out what I'm actually going to *do* about it.

Option One: I could try to fix this mess myself, but the only option would be to shave the whole lot pretty much bald, and there's no *way* I'm doing that.

Option Two: I could just walk around, proudly showing off my 'unique' style and hope that the 'attacked by hair-eating seagulls' look becomes popular. But something tells me I don't have quite the social currency to carry *that* one off.

You know, one of the good things about having lots of problems is that you get used to it – you get used to *trying* to solve them. My life is like a crash course in resilience, where every day, you either sink or swim. And you know what? I don't feel like sinking. Not just *yet* anyway.

Besides, I've got an *Option Three*, and I think it's a good one. I mean, what would *you* do if you had an absolute shocker of a haircut and not enough money to get it fixed?

You'd get a cheap hat. *Right?*

Twenty minutes later, I'm at the second-best charity shop in town, shuffling though their *very* limited collection of hats. And, sure, I *could* go to the animal sanctuary one, which is *way* better and even has some decent brands sometimes, but a couple of girls a bit older than me work in there at the weekends, so there's NO WAY I'm going there today – not looking like *this*.

So, yeah, I'm in here, where the only person who can judge me is this older lady behind the till, wearing some massive felt hat – maybe she tried to cut her own hair too? Besides, it's not like I can get anything that'll actually look good on me. It's *got* to be a beanie, otherwise you'd still see all the bald bits, and me and beanies don't get on too well.

Eventually I pick some snowboarding thing that would probably have been cool once – maybe thirty years ago?

On the plus side, the hat was really cheap, so as I walk out of the charity shop, I've still got some change rattling about in my pocket. I consider going to get a can of drink, but then change my mind, I'd better save it for when I get home – Dad'll need it for the food shopping.

Anyway, it's a nice day, you know? Cold but crisp and the sun's shining, so I forget about a drink and decide to walk back to Mum's along the river.

I like the river here; it calms me down, you know? The whispering, rippling sound of it, the way the light bends and glides over the water as it swirls around – it's kind of hypnotic. Also, there's this bridge that runs over it, some big old Victorian thing. Whenever it's raining and I need to get away from Mum and Greg, I come down here where it's dry and listen to music on my own.

I'm walking towards the bridge when I realise there's someone already there, leaning against the railings under the bridge. That's just typical – *seriously*, I don't ask for much – all I wanted was a place to sit down for a bit.

I'll just have to go on to the bench a bit further along. But as I get closer to the bridge, I realise that it's a whole group of lads. Older than me, maybe sixteen or so. Something like that. They look like they'd be in the sixth form, but they're not from my school. I don't recognise any of them.

My heart beats faster. I'm not getting a great feeling from them. You know how you can just tell, even from a distance? They're laughing, but it's not like *ha, ha, ha, what a funny joke* kind of laughing; it's a hard sound – as sharp as it's cold.

They've not seen me, so I head up the bank to my right, breaking through the trees and bushes, planning to skirt round the bridge, when something catches my attention. Actually I do recognise one of the voices in the group; it's a bit higher than the others. A bit younger.

Chris Tucker.

What's he doing here? I've never seen him *anywhere* near here before. I stop behind a broad tree and peer down the bank. From this angle I can just about see him and a couple of the lads under the bridge.

'Yeah, nice one, Si,' says Chris. 'I'll bet they didn't try *that* again!'

The group all laugh – that same jagged barking.

'Jesus! Don't be such a suck-up!' says a stocky lad whose face I can't see in the shadows.

'I wasn't,' protests Chris, his voice thinner and weaker than I've ever heard. 'I was just saying . . .'

'Yeah, well. No one's interested in what you're *saying*,' mimics the boy, 'Come on, Si, let's get out of here. I don't want to be hanging around under bridges in nowhere towns all day.'

Another figure slinks out from under the shadow of the bridge, sharp details sliding into view as he steps out from the darkness. He's wearing pristine white joggers, brand-new trainers and a baggy sweatshirt with a huge logo that I don't recognise but it's *obviously* expensive. His hair's cut close to his head, and the sunlight gleams off a huge watch on his wrist.

'Listen, Chris,' he says slowly, his voice low and

dangerous, 'you're only here because of your brother, *yeah*? But if you want to be more than John Tucker's baby brother, you've got to prove it. You know? You've got to *earn* it!'

'I can do it, Si,' says Chris. 'You *know* I can.'

Si puts his hands on Chris's shoulders, standing at least a head taller, probably more. His shoulders are broad and muscular – he looks how Chris Tucker *wants* to look.

'And Mo's right, *yeah*? There's no point coming out with all the chat. It's what you *do* that counts? You get me?'

Chris nods, silent.

'You're learning!' says Si.

Everyone laughs again and Chris's face reddens.

I can tell there's a lot riding on this moment, but I don't know what. For some reason I hold my breath, even though none of them would be able to hear me.

Si pauses as though he's considering something. Then he shakes his head and almost laughs. 'Okay, sure . . . why not, *right*?' He gestures to one of the other lads who comes out from under the bridge. 'You got the list, Tony?'

'Yeah.'

'Well, get Baby Tucker's number and message him the details – all of it. All the brands, the best places to get them – the whole lot.'

'Come on then,' mutters Tony. 'What's your number?'

I hear Chris giving Tony his phone number, his voice bright and artificially casual. There's a slight pause, then Chris's phone beeps and he looks down at the screen.

'You know what that list is, Baby Tucker?' asks Si quietly. 'It's kind of like a shopping list, okay?'

Chris nods.

'Good,' says Si. 'So if you get me everything on there . . . Well, if you get me *everything*, I'll give you a bloody Xbox myself – but *that's* not going to happen, so just get me everything that you *can* and then we'll come to some . . . *arrangement*. Okay?'

Chris nods again.

'Good lad,' says Si, putting his hands back on Chris's shoulders, holding so tight that I can see his knuckles whiten. 'And don't you tell *anyone*,' he adds in a low velvet growl. 'You hear? Not a *soul*. If you get caught, that's *your* problem.'

Chris sets his jaw and shakes his head. 'I won't get caught,' he says. 'And even if I *did*, I wouldn't say anything – I'm not an idiot!'

'Good lad!' says Si again, smiling. 'See, I'd hate for your brother to have to hear any . . . *upsetting* news about something bad happening to you.'

Si slaps Chris so hard on the shoulders that he stumbles forward, losing his balance and landing hard on his hand and knees.

'See you later, Baby Tucker,' calls Si as he walks away, his friends laughing as they follow him back under the shadow of the bridge and away.

I wait there a while. The last thing I want is to burst out of the bushes, right in the middle of *that* lot. I glance back down at Chris as he's scrambling up to his feet, wiping his hands on his jeans, shooting a look round to see if anyone saw.

I've got no idea what happens next . . .

Maybe I made some sort of noise. Stepped on a leaf or a twig or something. I don't know . . . but *something* makes Chris look up the bank directly towards me. Our eyes meet and I duck behind the tree, heart thudding sickeningly in my throat.

I wait there, silent, not moving. Not even breathing. After a few seconds, I hear footsteps as Chris walks away, back along the footpath away from me.

But the weird thing is, I'm *sure* that he saw me – I'd put money on it.

CHAPTER FOURTEEN

MUM PHONED ME AS I WAS WALKING home to ask if I wanted to meet her and Greg for lunch in town, but I passed on that idea, I mean, this weekend's already been about as Greg-filled as I can cope with. Besides, I knew that there was a pizza in the freezer, hot water in the radiators and a shelf full of DVDs back at the flat, so I settled down for a nice cosy afternoon.

As the day fades into the evening, a misty drizzle starts to fall, creating fuzzy halos round the street lights and, tell you what, I'm glad that I'm here, not at home in

the freezing flat with Dad. Then immediately I feel bad –
like I was being disloyal somehow.

It's about four thirty when I hear Mum and Greg
chatting in the hallway, so I spring up to grab the hat,
covering my 'haircut'.

The door opens and Mum and Greg bundle in, taking
off their damp coats and chatting away about the
exhibition and this old book Mum bought from a charity
shop, when suddenly there's this quiet *click*, and all the
lights and the TV cut out.

We stand there in the darkness.

'Looks like we need to feed the meter,' says Greg. 'God,
that thing gets hungry. Is there any change left?'

'So, *about that* . . .' says Mum. 'I needed it the other
day for the shopping. Sorry.'

'Not to worry,' says Greg, putting his coat back on. 'I
fancied a walk anyway.'

Mum turns to me and touches my arm. 'Will? Be a love
and nip to the shop, would you?'

I kind of shrug but don't really say anything, while

Mum rummages in a drawer, opening a tin and pulling out a ten-pound note. 'Get some change for the meter, and you can get a can of Coke too, if you like?'

'What, the *real* stuff?' I ask. 'Not some knock-off?'

'You still like it, don't you?'

I grin, and I'm pretty much out of the door before Mum's finished saying, 'Thanks, love!'

I choose a playlist on my phone and the music throbs out of the headphones. Walking quickly, I try to keep my feet moving in time with the music, as though it's a game. It's hardly any distance to the shop, five minutes tops. But by the time I push the door open with a *ding*, the drizzle's made up its mind to get serious and turn into rain, so my hood's kind of clinging to the side of my hat. And yeah, I know that a hat AND a hood's kind of weird, but I need to keep the hat dry so I can wear it later.

'Bit wet out?' asks the guy behind the counter without looking up from his phone.

'Yeah, a bit wet,' I reply, and he nods.

Now that is some CLASSIC small talk. *Seriously* next-level stuff.

I walk round to the fridge and take out the chilled shiny red can. I feel like the hero in some computer game quest. If there was no one around, I'd probably feel tempted to hold the can up in the air and hum some triumphant bit of music. I LOVE this stuff. But Mr Chatty behind the till is there, so I don't do that. I definitely imagine it, though.

I take the can over to the till and hold out the tenner. Without looking up from his phone, the guy takes hold of the note, opens the till, and tries to pass me a fiver and some change.

'Sorry, but can I have it *all* as change, please?' I ask.

Mr Chatty sighs and points to a sign that reads no change given without a purchase, muttering, 'I spend half my life giving out change!'

'To be fair, this *is* a purchase . . .' I protest, holding up the can and kind of waggling it about.

'Cheapest thing you could get!' he retorts.

'*Hardly,*' I say. 'I mean, it's not like this stuff's CHEAP, is it? Not in here anyway. I could go a bit further up the road and buy it from the supermarket for, like, half the price.'

Mr Chatty puts his phone down and glances over at me. 'You've got a cheek!' he says, but he's smiling, 'Look, it's fine, I'll do you the change. Don't want to be responsible for you drowning in the rain on the walk to Asda.'

'Thanks!' I say and I smile back. Suddenly I feel a bit like me and Mr Chatty are kind of friends.

'Besides,' he adds, 'hardly had anyone in all evening. Every little helps, right?'

'Tell me about it!' I say, half laughing but unable to keep the bitterness out of my voice.

He looks at me again and I feel like this time he's *really* looking at me. Taking in the jeans that were old when we got them from the charity shop, the black school shoes, the soaking-wet hoody and the old-fashioned hat.

He nods to himself, takes out the change and passes it to me. 'Here you go,' he says. 'Cheers then.'

'Thanks,' I say, taking the change and counting it out

as I walk towards the door.

I turn back. 'You've given me too much,' I say. 'This is a tenner's worth of change.'

'I can count,' he replies, catching my eye and smiling. 'Now, you get going, before you have to *swim* home!'

Kindness is weird. It can feel like being knocked off balance – especially *unexpected* kindness.

'Thanks,' I say as I open the door. 'Seriously . . . *thanks*!'

'No worries,' he replies with a grin, and then as the door closes with a *ding* he shouts, 'That stuff'll rot your teeth, mind!'

CHAPTER FIFTEEN

OUTSIDE, I START RUNNING. I can feel the rain creeping down between my shoulder blades, but I'm grinning all the same, trying to run as smoothly as possible so I don't shake up the drink too much.

I'm just turning on to Mum's road, when my sole slips on the wet paving and I stumble forward. There's this weird confused moment, when I've got no idea what's happening and I feel like I'm about to *totally* pile it, but somehow I just about manage to stay on my feet.

As I skid to a halt, my headphones fall from my ears. I hear a rattling, skittering sound, and watch my phone bouncing across the ground, casting a pale dancing light across the rain-soaked pavement, until it slips over the kerb and into a deep puddle. The light vanishes.

Scrambling forward, I kneel down and fish about in the puddle. After a second or two I feel my phone and pull it out. The screen is totally blank. There's nothing coming out of the headphones and the whole thing just looks dead.

You ever hear the phrase *take one step forward, two steps back*?

That's how I feel. Except it's more like take two steps backwards, then *another* two, then you might as well just run backwards as fast as you can and keep on going.

It's like my whole life's going *backwards* – all the time.

My eyes shut tight. My teeth grind together. Every muscle in my body tenses.

It's not fair.

Nothing is fair.

NOTHING!

A huge black hole of anger opens around me, swallowing all the goodness of the world – consuming everything – until there's nothing left, and I just *exist* in the middle of this huge swirling rage storm.

I don't know how long it lasts, but when the feeling

fades I'm left standing in the rain. Soaking wet and cold. Without the furious heat of the anger there's nothing left. *I'm* nothing. Just an empty shell.

I walk back to Mum's and ring the buzzer.

'Hey, Will! That was quick!' comes Greg's cheery voice through the intercom and I hear the door unlock.

I climb up the stairs and into the flat. In the light from the hallway I can just about see my hand as it reaches out and places the coins down on the table. Then my hands take off my hoody and hang that up on the coat rack. I hear water drip on to the floor.

'Hey, are you all right, Will?' asks Greg from somewhere far away.

I nod.

'Look, give me a second . . .'

There is the sound of coins being put into the meter and then the lights come on.

'Hooray!' cheers Mum from inside the bathroom. 'Well done, Will! Is it all right with you two if I stay in the bath a while? I've not had a proper soak in *ages*, and it's really nice in here with all the candles. I might even put some music on.'

'That's fine, love,' calls Greg as music starts playing from the bathroom. 'You take as long as you like.'

When he turns to me, his face drops. 'What's *happened*?' he asks, his voice quieter and lower than usual.

I don't say anything – I just stand there all blank and empty.

'Come on, Will,' insists Greg. '*Please!* At least dry yourself off a bit. You're soaking!' Greg picks up a towel from the airer and throws it over to me, but everything's moving too fast, or I'm moving in slow motion, and the towel just drops to the floor.

Greg grabs it and leads me over to the sofa. Pulling my soaking hat off, he puts it on the radiator and starts drying my hair with the towel. 'So . . .' he says, 'what happened?'

'Nothing . . .' I mutter. '*Everything*. I don't want to talk about it.'

Greg's towelling stops for a moment. 'Is it the hair?'

'Said I don't want to talk about it.'

'Fair enough,' says Greg, 'but, look, I can try and sort the hair out a bit, if you like?'

I shrug. Like that'll help, like that's going to change anything.

Greg gets some scissors from the kitchen. 'Lean forward,' he says.

I lean forward.

Damp clumps of hair begin to fall, gathering by my feet, by my shoes – my *awful* shoes – and I start to cry. Huge gulping sobs that I try to suppress, just like I try to suppress *everything*. Silent heart-ripping sobs.

'*Hey* . . . come on, Will,' says Greg, putting a hand on my shoulder. 'Look, I know that things are tough, but we're here for you – *I'm* here for you – if you want me to be. I swear I can *try* to help.'

'But you *can't*!' I cough out between sobs. '*No one* can. That's the problem! *Everything's* bad. All of it. My whole life is ruined. Messed up – the whole *lot*.'

Greg says nothing but keeps silently cutting my hair.

'I know what you mean,' he says eventually. 'I know how that feels.'

I snort to myself. *As if* . . . Greg? With his stupid extended *'he-llllo'* and his stupid jolly face. I turn round, my face feeling all twisted up, but when I look at Greg I see him differently. He's smiling but it's kind of a sad smile, and somehow I can tell that he *does* know what I mean, that he *has* felt what I'm feeling.

'Dropped my phone . . .' I add, pulling the dead lump of glass, metal and plastic out of my pocket. 'It went in a puddle.'

'Pass it here,' says Greg, holding his hand out. 'Did you try to turn it on again?'

I shake my head. 'What's the point? It's dead, isn't it?'

'Maybe. Maybe not . . .' replies Greg. 'But it's a good job you didn't try to turn it on. Sometimes *that's* what completely ruins them.'

He takes the phone and walks into the kitchen. Curious, despite myself, I watch as he opens the cupboard and takes out a Tupperware container. He fills it with dried rice and buries the phone in it, then he closes the lid tight.

'The rice sucks out all the moisture, see? But make sure you leave it like that for a couple of days, and *don't* try to turn it on. Okay?'

'You think it'll work?' I ask.

Greg shrugs. 'I don't know. It's worth trying, right?'

'I *suppose* . . .' I say. 'I didn't have any data or credit anyway. I basically just have it for music.'

Greg's face lights up. 'Well, you know what? I think I *can* help with that!'

He goes through into the box room – *my* room. Normally I'd feel weird about him being in there when I'm staying over, but right now I don't mind. I hear boxes being moved about and a minute or so later I hear him say, '*Ah!* There you are!'

He comes back in, holding up this weird little box with headphones attached to it. 'It's a Walkman!' he says. 'You know? Like a portable tape player? Well, it's a recorder as well, actually. We used to record our rehearsals on it, back when I was in the band.'

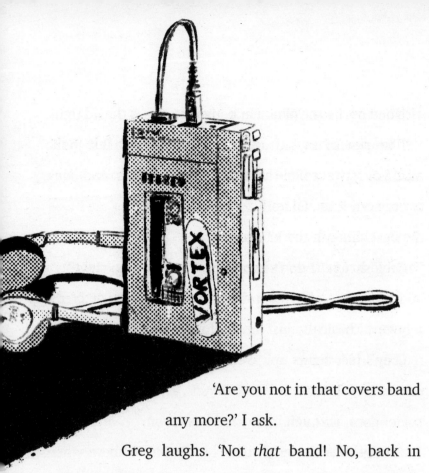

'Are you not in that covers band any more?' I ask.

Greg laughs. 'Not *that* band! No, back in my twenties.' He pauses and smiles. 'We were pretty good – got a few features in the *NME*.'

'*Shut up!*' I say, properly interested now.

'Yeah.' Greg nods. 'We came number one in their top five unsigned bands one time.' He grins, as he passes me the Walkman. 'Seriously, I thought we had it made. We played a whole load of gigs, supported all the big acts at the time, recorded a few demos. Nearly got signed.'

'No way!' I say. 'What happened?'

'*I* happened!' says Greg. 'I made some mistakes. Well, a LOT of mistakes.' He shakes his head. 'You know, I was twenty-one and suddenly everyone was telling me I was the best thing in the world.' He looks at me and shrugs. 'Trouble is, I *believed* them and started acting like a total idiot! *Then*, after a few months of me acting up, I had a huge blowout with Jake, our lead guitarist, and left the band just before we were due onstage at a big gig. I ruined *everything*! I remember yelling that I didn't need any of them and would do better on my own.'

Greg gestures around his small living room. 'As you can see . . . it didn't quite turn out that way.'

'Wow . . .' I whisper. 'I'm sorry . . .'

What's weird is that he grins here, like an *actual* proper smile.

'Nothing to be sorry about!' he says. '*Firstly,* it was a long time ago. And *secondly,* if we'd ended up being some huge famous band, then I'd never have had the chance to grow in the way that I have. You know?'

He pauses, and sits down on a chair in front of me. 'The thing is, I'd put *everything* on that future, on the band, and when it didn't happen I was crushed.' He looks me in the eye. '*Genuinely* crushed. But since then I've learned a lot. I've learned how to be happy, which I never was before. And besides, I've still got my music. You know, I can sit down anytime I like to play and it costs me *nothing*! Plus, it's the life I've led, which meant that I got to meet your mum, and right now I genuinely think that if the band had gone on to be HUGE, I wouldn't be as happy as I am now.'

'You mean . . . you'd be *happier*?' I say, but I smile to show that I'm joking.

'Ha!' Greg grins and pretends to slap me across the head. 'Seriously, though, Will, what I'm saying is that I know that life can feel rough. Maybe even unbearable sometimes –' he puts his hand on my shoulder – 'but so long as you DO bear it, as long as you find a way through each bad moment, and the next one, and the next, and you just keep going, then *eventually* you can look back, and then? The pain's nowhere near as sharp. See, eventually *all* those bad moments are just small steps on a much bigger journey. They don't have to define you. Do you see what I mean?'

'Just keep going?' I say.

'Pretty much!' replies Greg, grinning.

That's when we hear the bathroom door opening.

Greg jumps up to grab my beanie and throws it over to me. 'Look, I've done my best,' he says, 'but I'm no miracle worker. Best put this back on to avoid any questions from your mum!' He scuffs all the cut hair under the sofa. 'I'll tidy that up later!'

'Thanks, Greg,' I say. 'You know, for *everything*.'

'Think nothing of it,' he says.

But I do. I think a lot of it.

CHAPTER SIXTEEN

So, yeah, that was quite the plot twist. I had *literally* never imagined that I'd end up liking Greg, but there you are. I guess it just goes to show that sometimes the world *really can* surprise you.

After all that, I actually had the best time that I've ever had round at Mum's. We had lasagne with garlic bread for tea and I drank my can of Coke, then we all watched a film together, and it was good. You know, properly relaxing. Mum *did* ask why I was wearing the hat the whole time, but Greg chipped in to say that he thought it was cool, so Mum just shrugged it off.

It was like that the next day too. Greg dug out some of his old tapes; he's got some decent stuff. You know, *obviously* it was all nineties, but, still, there's a whole bunch of albums and bands I'd never heard of. Plenty to keep me going till my phone dries out anyway.

The next day they both walk me to the bus stop. Mum pulls me into a hug. 'Say "hi" to your dad for me,' she says.

'Will do,' I reply, giving her an extra-tight squeeze. 'I love you, Mum.'

'I love you too!' she says, squeezing me back.

I smile at her as I turn to Greg. 'Thanks for letting me stay over,' I say, even though I've never said anything like that before. Mum sort of does this funny blink, like she's trying not to look *too* surprised.

'No worries,' says Greg, holding out a battered old tape box. 'Oh yeah, by the way, here's a tape of demos we recorded.' He leans in closer as he passes me the tape and whispers, 'And something to sort out the hair too!'

'What's going on with you two?' asks Mum. 'It's like

151

you're both school kids, whispering together!'

'Ah, it's nothing!' says Greg. 'Just a bit of an in-joke.'

Mum shakes her head and does the blinking thing again. 'You two have *in-jokes* now?'

I grin at her, then turn back to Greg. 'I meant to ask, what was your band called?'

There's a pause. Mum smirks.

'Vortex,' says Greg eventually.

'*Vortex?*' I say.

Greg grins. 'Come on, I said we were a good *band* – I didn't say we had a good name!'

Just then the bus arrives. 'I'll definitely have a listen,' I say, patting the tape as I climb on board the bus. And I mean it. I will.

I walk to the back of the bus, brushing my hands lightly along the seat backs and sit down. Then I put on the headphones over my hat and wave goodbye to Mum and Greg as the bus pulls slowly away. While I'm taking the tape out of the box, I can see a tenner tucked inside. *Nice one, Greg!* I can get the whole hair mess properly sorted out now. It'll be too late by the time I get home, but after school on Monday should be all right – so long as I can get into town in time.

I put the tape in the player the way Greg showed me, rewind it and press play. You know what? Greg's right. Vortex were good. Like, *really* good. They had this sort of shoegaze thing going on, but with really hard guitars and loads of synths and samplers and stuff. And, tell you what, he can sing. I mean, I knew Greg could *sing* sing, because Mum's taken me to some of his covers band gigs. But on these demos, on the songs that he'd written *himself*, it all just . . . *works*. And despite what Greg says about finding personal happiness vs fame, fortune, mansions, yachts and a massive ego, I still think it's a shame his band never happened. But there we go – that's life, I guess?

I'm sat there on the bus, letting the world slide away past the window as I listen to the music, each stop and start of the bus drifting by, when suddenly I feel a tap on my shoulder. I turn round, pulling the headphones off my ears.

My eyes widen. It's Chris Tucker and he's sitting on the seat across the aisle from me.

'You all right?' he asks.

I nod my head. 'Yeah, you?'

'Yeah, all right.' He gestures over his shoulder.

'So what you doin' in that dump of a town?'

'My mum lives there,' I say. 'What about you?'

He looks at me and doesn't say anything for a long time. 'My brother's got a place there,' he replies eventually.

I nod slowly. 'Right.'

I don't mention anything about seeing him down by the river, and he doesn't mention it either.

'What you listening to, then?' he asks.

'Music,' I reply.

'Yeah, *obviously*! I mean, I know you're weird, but I didn't think you'd be listening to . . . *like* . . .' He pauses, obviously trying to think of something funny to say and failing. 'What are those headphones? They look ancient.'

I shrug. 'Yeah, it's this old Walkman I borrowed. My phone died, see?'

Chris nods. 'Nightmare. Let's have a look then?' He holds his hand out.

I hesitate. I mean, this is Chris Tucker. But something about him seems different today. You know, for a start he's not called me Poundland, and actually he's not said or done anything out of order – not *yet* anyway.

Wondering if I'm going to regret it, I take the Walkman out of my pocket and pass it over.

'Jesus! What is *that*?' he says. 'You been time-travelling or something?'

'I told you it was old,' I say. 'My mum's bloke lent it to me. It's pretty sweet actually; you can record with it too.'

'Right,' says Chris, clearly not interested as he passes the Walkman back to me. 'Can't play *Demonlance*, though, can it?'

'Nope, no games – just the music.'

But something about his question catches me by surprise. See, *Demonlance* is this really involved RPG game – it's *total* D&D stuff.

'So, what? You play *Demonlance*?' I ask, wondering if he's trying to wind me up.

'*Sometimes . . .*' he replies, cagey now. 'How about you?'

'It wouldn't work on my phone,' I say, 'but, you know, I like the look of it.'

'Yeah, it's decent,' he says, then he nods to me, like that's the end of the conversation. 'See you later then, Will,' he adds and puts his own headphones back in.

Will? Chris Tucker just called me Will. Like, my *real* name. Not some stupid nickname or my surname or anything like that – he called me *Will*.

I think I must be doing my mum's fast-blinking thing, so I just mutter, 'Yeah, cheers then, Chris,' and put my headphones back on too, wondering what sort of parallel world I've slid into where Chris Tucker talks to me like we're mates.

I press play on the Walkman and carry on working my way through more of Vortex's lost demo tape. Seriously, there are, like, five or six absolute gems on here, and

Tree, car, house, tree, pylon, sign, car, house, tree, owl...

another four or five that are solid too. In fact, I wouldn't skip *any* of them, which is good, because it takes ages to fast-forward through a song on this thing! Anyway, you know what? I think Vortex have found their first new fan in quite some time – I'll have to tell Greg when I see him next.

As the bus glides in and out of villages, fields and woodland, I let my eyes drift over the passing landscape, almost sliding out of focus, barely registering what's going past.

Tree, car, house, tree, pylon, sign, car, house, hill, tree, owl . . . OWL? What?

I spin my head round and, sure enough, rising up from a branch on the edge of this small wood is a huge silvery owl – massive wings slicing through the air as she soars up into the sky where she's almost immediately lost from view.

I don't know how I could tell you that I know, but even just in that snap-second, even from that distance, I just *know* without the slightest doubt that it was the same owl.

This warm soft glow spreads through me, melting all the bitter shards that I hadn't even realised were there, and I lean back against my seat, smiling as the music plays on.

She was real – I *know* she was real.

CHAPTER SEVENTEEN

HERE WE ARE, THEN . . . BACK in school on Monday morning.

Usually I'd be kind of down at the whole idea, especially with the whole row with Cameron and the haircut disaster, but I've got my trusty hat pulled down low, and I don't know why I just feel all right today. Dad was in a decent mood when I got in. He's still waiting to hear about that job interview, but he reckons it's basically a formality, which means he thinks it's in the bag. And if the Chris Tucker-shaped thorn in my side is going to be less pointy, then that's a good thing too, right? Plus, we've got Art just before lunch, so I only have a couple of other lessons to get through first.

When I walk into the art room, Mr Prince is standing up by the board, trying to get the projector to work. With loads of teachers, everyone would just sit and watch, kind of enjoying the show, but with Mr Prince there's, like, five kids trying to help him get it all working – *everyone* likes Mr Prince.

There's a sudden flash of light and an image fills the screen. Mr Prince cheers, grinning as he looks around the room. Everyone's smiling – it's like everyone just *wants* Mr Prince's lessons to go well, so they do. It's weird what can make or break an atmosphere.

'I have some exciting news today,' says Mr Prince. 'There's a national wildlife art competition coming up, and there's an eleven to fifteen section. It can be any medium you like – photograph, drawing, painting, sculpture, textiles, digital art, whatever – it just needs to celebrate nature and wildlife.'

'Cool,' mutter a few kids, but there's not a great deal of excitement in the room.

'The winner and ten runners-up will get their work shown at a gallery in London *and* have an all-expenses-paid trip to go to the exhibition . . .' continues Mr Prince.

There's *definitely* more interest now. An all-expenses-paid trip to London? That's pretty sweet! I mean, apart from going to my mum's I've not been more than ten miles from my home in, well . . . *years*.

'Not to mention a two-hundred-and-fifty-pound cash prize for the winner and vouchers for art supplies for each runner-up.' Mr Prince nods slowly. 'Not a bad prize, I'm sure you'll agree?'

That's done it. Suddenly the room is on fire, with lots of people chattering excitedly to each other. I feel a giddy swirling in my stomach. Winning £250? Just *imagine*!

'Okay, okay!' says Mr Prince, laughing as he holds his hands in the air. 'You have to *win it* before you can spend it! But I'm mentioning this because I know some of you in here would have a *very* real chance.'

He catches my eye here. It's subtle, so that no one else would notice, but I *know* that he's talking to me. 'Some of you have got some excellent wildlife work, and I would *strongly* recommend that you enter. I'll leave all the details up on the screen so you can log on and fill in all the required forms. For everyone else who would like to enter, but doesn't have any wildlife work, I'm going to make this lesson and the next one available for the competition, so you should have enough time to come up a with a piece that you're happy with.'

While everyone's getting their materials out and chatting about what they're planning to do, Mr Prince comes over to me. 'How about it, Will?' he asks. 'You'll be entering, won't you?'

'Definitely,' I say. 'I just need to get hold of a camera; my phone's dead.'

Mr Prince nods. 'I can help, if you like? We can use one of the digital cameras here, so you get a *really* crisp image. Give you as good a chance as possible. We can do it next lesson, if you like. Does that sound good?'

'*Definitely!*' I say again, nodding. 'Thanks, sir.'

See, that's what's so great about Mr Prince. It's like he just *gets* it. He gets me and everything that's going on. When he helps out, it's just easy, you know, natural, like he's just doing me a favour so I don't feel like a charity case.

Thinking about this makes me think of Cameron and I feel bad. I mean, yeah, he was a bit heavy-handed, and he *totally* got it wrong, trying to pretend that those shoes didn't fit him or whatever, but he was only trying to help. He was only trying to do me a favour. I decide to sort things out with him the next chance I get.

We all pile into the hall after lunch for assembly. The head's up on the stage and his army of deputies are all there in EXTRA-stern mode. There's obviously something serious going on.

'This assembly was *meant* to focus on general health and well-being,' begins the head, peering out from beneath wiry rutted brows, 'but unfortunately I have to discuss another matter instead. It has become apparent that a pair of running shoes has been stolen. The locker they were kept in has been forced open, so not only has there been a theft but criminal damage has been caused.'

He glares around the room. 'I'm sure I do not need to remind most of you that such behaviour is completely unacceptable!' He slams his fist down on his desk here, and, do you know what, I think he *really* is angry, not just *pretend-teacher-angry*.

After a pause he carries on. 'The training shoes in question were, I believe, a particularly expensive pair. Not, of course, that this has any bearing on the matter, as regardless of monetary value theft of *any* sort is intolerable in our community!'

The head *always* speaks like this; that's why assemblies go on for so long.

'Needless to say,' continues the head, 'the culprit *will* be found, and it would be advisable for them to return the training shoes to the staffroom. If this was just an ill-considered prank and the shoes are returned by the end of the day, then Cameron Romelle's parents have informed me they will take the matter no further and will not, on this occasion, contact the police.'

Well, *that* really gets my attention; it's *Cameron's* shoes that have been stolen! His brand-new, insanely rare, almost one-of-a-kind shoes. I shake my head slowly as the head's face darkens and he continues. 'The damage to the locker, however, is another matter *entirely . . .'*

After that I kind of zone out. Cameron must be losing it! I mean, those trainers cost an absolute fortune! And, yeah, his parents are pretty chill, but they are *not* going to be happy about this! I look around the hall but I can't see Cameron anywhere. Still, we've got Geography together next, so I'll catch up with him in there. It'll give me a chance to patch things up with him too.

As per every other lesson we've had since *The Big Bad Row,* Cameron's not sitting by me in Geography. I'm at the desk behind him. So it's kind of tricky to get his attention. I wait until the lesson's well underway and we're doing this group discussion thing. I lean forward and tap Cameron on the back. He turns and looks at me, eyes red-rimmed and sore-looking.

'Mate,' I whisper, 'I just wanted to say that I'm really sorry to hear abou—'

'*William Pinker!*' shouts Mr Fraser.

God, I *hate* it when people do that. You know? Use the long version of your first name *and* your surname. It's SO unnecessary. I mean, there's not even anyone else called Will in this class. Plus, I hate my surname, so yeah . . . there's that too.

'I thought I had instructed everyone to discuss this quietly in their table groups?' adds Mr Fraser.

'Yes, *sir*,' I say. 'Sorry, *sir*.'

Now, I swear that I didn't *mean* to make it sound bad, but I guess I was feeling irritated by the whole *William Pinker* thing, so I might have had a bit of a face on.

'I will *NOT* stand for that tone!' bellows Mr Fraser, eyes flaring dangerously. 'And why are you wearing that *ridiculous* hat? Take it off immediately.'

I sit there feeling sick.

Greg had done an *okayish* job patching up my hair but there was still a bald strip right up the side – it's still pretty bad. So taking the hat off wasn't high up on my list of Top Ten Things That I'd Love to Do Right Now. To be honest, it wasn't even in the top 100.

Freeze time and run away or maybe *Fall through a wormhole to literally anywhere else* were definitely strong contenders for the top spot, though.

'Sorry, sir,' I mutter. 'I can't do that . . .'

'You *can't do that*?' he explodes, coughing out a short sharp laugh. 'And would you care to explain to us WHY you are incapable of removing that hat?'

Everyone's looking at me now. I feel my cheeks flush as the sick feeling grows.

'Maybe it's been glued on?' adds Mr Fraser.

A few kids kind of laugh here. You know things are bad when the class sides with a teacher over you.

'It's not *that*, sir,' I say, using my best, most reasonable good-student voice. 'It's just that, you know, I sort of can't. Like . . . I'd rather not.' I nod slightly to myself.

Hopefully that'll do the trick.

'Well, *Mr* Pinker . . .' says Mr Fraser in an overly syrupy voice, 'I'm sure that you might *rather not*. Just as I'd *rather not* waste everyone's time, dealing with disruptive irritating students and yet *here we are*!' He almost shouts those last words. Then he looks me dead in the eye. 'Now . . . Take. The. Hat. *Off!*'

Everyone's looking at me now. I mean, what can I do? I can continue to refuse and get, like, a bunch of new negatives that absolutely WILL go back to Dad or I can take the hat off and have everyone rip it out of me.

My hands feel as sweaty as my mouth is dry. I look over at Mr Fraser, silently pleading with him not to do this.

'Mr Pinker!' he bellows. 'Take it OFF!'

'Fine!' I yell back. 'If it means SO much to you!' I yank the hat off and hurl it across the room. There's this sudden gasping sound and a moment's silence before the laughing starts.

'What is THAT!?'

'Sick haircut, mate!'

'Yeah, sick. Where'd you get it done? Just so I can *never* go there!'

All I can hear is everyone laughing – laughing at me.

A familiar heat flares up in me and everything's throbbing with this red violent pulsing. Mr Fraser's yelling at the class, but it's not working – you can't fight fire with fire.

I stand up, almost flinging my seat backwards. It skids across the floor. I don't care. I've got to get out of here. *Now*. I need to get away. Away from *everything*. If there was a way I could just disappear, just stop existing, I'd do it. Without a second's thought.

'*Everyone!*' shouts Mr Fraser. '*Quiet!* Be quiet NOW! And, *Will* . . . come on, come back, sit down –' His tone's different now – like he's realising that this hasn't played out *quite* how he thought it would.

But it's too late. It's played out exactly how I knew it would. Everyone's laughing. They think I'm a joke – and I am. I *know* I am. But, I tell you what, it hurts all the same. I grab my bag and rush blindly for the door.

Cameron is looking at me – soft brown eyes wide and full of pity. I grit my teeth, pushing the feeling back, but it's that look that does it – the pity – *that's* what tips me over the edge.

Tears start falling. I run out of the room, vision blurred,

eyes streaming. I'm furious. Furious with Mr Fraser for starting this all off. Furious with Cameron for his pity. Furious with the class for laughing.

Furious with the whole world.

CHAPTER EIGHTEEN

SO THAT WAS IT. I just left. Straight out of the school gates and I kept on walking until I found myself in the old graveyard. At least most people here are dead – they tend to be less hassle.

'Hey! *Will!*' a voice calls out.

I shake my head. *Seriously? Who's this?*

I shoot a look back, mouth clamped so tightly shut it feels like my teeth might shatter. I'm *not* in the mood to talk. It's Kalia.

'Hey! Come on, wait up!' she calls out.

'What are you doing here? Shouldn't you be in school?'

'Shouldn't *you*?' she asks, raising one eyebrow.

'Well, yeah, but . . .' I begin. Then I realise that my

eyes must be totally bloodshot, I've probably got snot all down my face and my hair's . . . well, my hair's my hair. I fall silent, and stare at the ground.

'I saw you running out of school,' says Kalia, stepping towards me, her hand touching my arm. 'Looks like you're in a bit of a mess.'

'And you just came after me?' I ask, my brain not quite coping with this information. 'But *why*? Won't you get in trouble?'

'I guess,' she says, shrugging. 'As for *why*, it's because you look like you need a hand. *Right?*'

I mean, sure, I could *say* I'm fine. I could pretend that everything's okay. But it's not, *is it*? Nowhere near.

'Yeah,' I say, nodding slowly. Tears start flowing again but this time I let them. 'It's just all so messed up! *Everything!*'

Kalia gestures over to a bench against a wall. We sit down, saying nothing for a bit.

'Mr Prince showed us your owl picture,' Kalia says after a while.

'*What?*' I say. That wasn't what I'd been expecting her to say.

She nods. 'Yeah, he was chatting about some exhibition competition. Said your painting was an example of the standard we should be aiming for. The way I see it, there's no point *anyone* else entering if you've done that. *You know?*' She looks at me. 'That painting's amazing, Will.'

'Cheers . . .' I mutter, looking down.

She tilts her head towards me and looks at me from under her eyebrows. 'So it's not like *everything's* bad, is it?'

'Yeah, well, maybe,' I say, 'but everything *else* is.'

Kalia nods. 'I mean, sure . . . your hair could do with a *teeny* bit of attention.'

Caught by surprise, I almost laugh. 'You *think*?'

She narrows her eyes and pretends to inspect my hair. 'Yessss, I think you might have missed a bit here . . .' She holds up one of the longer, messier strands.

I laugh fully now. 'I was going to get it sorted after

school,' I say, shrugging. 'See, I'd been wearing this hat, and everything was fine until Mr Fraser got all *RESPECT MY AUTHORITY* and made me take it off. Then . . . well, to be honest, I don't really know what happened. It was a bit of a blur.'

'Well, that's Mr Fraser for you,' says Kalia. 'You should have *known* not to push anything with him! But, look, it's all done now, just forget about it.'

'But everyone was laughing at me!' I say. *'Everyone!'*

Kalia nods. 'Yeah, I've had that. I was in Year Six when we first moved here, and these lads down the road from me used to do this hula-dancing thing ALL THE TIME. You know my dad's from Hawaii, right?'

I shake my head.

'Well, he is,' says Kalia. 'He moved to London for work in his twenties, and for some reason stayed. Well, I guess that reason was my mum. All the same –' she gestures up at the mottled concrete sky and scrubby grass in the graveyard – 'would it have killed them to both move back to Hawaii once they'd met?'

'What's it like,' I ask, 'Hawaii?'

'Never been,' says Kalia, shrugging. 'I'd love to but we can't afford it. So, yeah . . . I'd ask these kids to stop, but they wouldn't. If anything, that just made it worse. Then they had something to aim for, you know?'

I nod. Like I said about Chris Tucker, some people can sniff out your weak point from miles away.

Kalia continues. 'So when people like those idiots do the hula dancing to mock me or wear grass skirts and put on stupid plastic flowers at fancy-dress parties, it's like that's all I am to them – *fancy dress*.' Her lips purse together and her eyes narrow.

'So how did you stop it in the end,' I ask, 'the hula dancing?'

I can imagine her squaring up to them, quietly confident, defying them to carry on.

'I cried,' she says.

'Oh . . .'

'And when I went home, still crying, Dad told me that they probably just didn't know any better, so I did a presentation at my primary school about Dad's ancestral history and what it means to us as a family.' She nods. 'That pretty much did the trick.'

'Pretty much?'

'Well, there was this one kid who kept it up,' she says. 'Isaac Richards.'

'And what did you do about *him*?'

She looks at me and grins, revealing sharp white teeth. 'I waited until the end of the day when he was walking home on his own. I took his pencil case off him and slowly snapped every pencil right in front of him. Didn't say a word as I did it. Then I told him that if he carried on, it'd be his arm next.'

I laugh. 'I knew it!'

Kalia's laughing too. 'Well, you know, as a *rule* I don't really condone aggression.'

'Ha! Nice one.'

'No, seriously,' says Kalia. 'Look, there's a difference between aggression and making it clear that you're not going to be pushed around, right?'

'I guess . . .' I say, although *really*? How would *I* know?

'So, look, don't worry about today. You know school . . . there'll be some other drama for everyone to chat about in a day or two. You just need to feel good about YOU, okay?'

She's right about school; it's a constant merry-go-round of drama – nothing ever sticks for long.

'And as far as your hair goes,' continues Kalia, 'save your money. My brother's training to be a barber, and he's good – seriously. Come round to mine and he'll sort it out for nothing; he wants all the practice he can get. He'll be there now, if you like?'

'What about school?'

Kalia looks at her phone. 'There's only another twenty minutes left. By the time we got there, it'll be time to leave or just go to detention.' She shrugs. 'Look, we'll deal with the fallout tomorrow, *okay*?' She stands up and looks over at me, smiling. 'So you coming then?'

Slowly I stand up and nod. I mean, of course I do.

Wouldn't you?

CHAPTER NINETEEN

'MATE! WHO'S RESPONSIBLE FOR this?' asks Lani, Kalia's brother. He's older than her. Seventeen or so, I'd guess? He peers closely at my hair, but although he's smiling, I can tell he's not being harsh.

'Kind of a joint effort,' I say. 'Me and my mum's bloke. The clippers broke while I was doing it. He tried to tidy it up, but, yeah . . . it didn't work out too well.'

'I can see . . .' says Lani. 'Anyway, nothing that a fade can't fix. I'll have to take it pretty high, though. That okay with you?'

'Anything that isn't *this* is okay with me!' I say, gesturing at the mess on my head.

'Good lad!' he says, tucking a tea towel round my collar to keep the hair out. Then he turns on the clippers. 'Right, let's get to work.'

Kalia sprawls back on an armchair, her legs dangling over the arm as she watches her brother cut my hair. Their living room's not much bigger than ours, but it feels *totally* different. I can smell something cooking, a sweet, spicy scent. They've got pictures up on the wall, paintings, photos, drawings, clay models that Kalia and her brothers must have made when they were kids, and there are plants growing pretty much everywhere. It feels alive – like a home.

Lani and Kalia chat easily to each other as he works, gently teasing each other but affectionate, and I feel totally at ease, which is weird, considering that, really, I've only just met both of them.

It's hard to explain. They just have a good *feeling* about them. You know? Calm. Every time I've seen her in school, Kalia seems hard, sort of defensive, but right now, at home, her body language is totally relaxed.

I zone out a bit, the soft murmur of their voices and the clippers creating a soothing wash of sound that carries the time away without me even noticing.

'You can stay for dinner, if you like?' says Kalia.

'Who me?' I reply.

'Well, yeah . . .' she says. 'Lani kind of lives here already, being my brother and everything. Of *course* I mean you. Mum's left a stew in the slow cooker; there'll be plenty.'

She stands up and walks round the chair I'm sat in, inspecting my hair. 'Told you he'd do a good job.'

'Yeah. I'm not one to brag,' says Lani, tilting my head to one side and then another, making a few last small adjustments, 'but that IS a whole load better.'

He pulls the tea towel out from round my neck and nods towards the hallway. 'Go and take a look.' I glance over at him and he grins. 'Third door along.'

'Come on!' says Kalia, laughing. She grabs my shoulders and steers me into their small bathroom. I can see her in the mirror; she's smiling, her eyes bright as she gestures towards someone almost unrecognisable in the mirror. 'What do you think?'

'That's just . . .' I murmur, my eyes prickling. 'It's . . . it's *brilliant*. I look totally different.'

'Mm-hmm.' Kalia nods. '*Definitely* an improvement.'

'You like?' asks Lani, peering in round the door.

'I love it!' I say. 'I don't know what to say!'

'Well, "thank you" is customary,' says Kalia, but she's smiling.

'Yeah, *yeah* . . . of course!' I turn to face Lani. '*Thank you!* Seriously.'

'No worries,' he says, grinning as he turns to leave. 'Any time, Will. It's all good practice.'

I turn my head slowly from side to side, looking in the mirror. It's cropped tight to my head on the sides and then fades up into a number four and from there to about two inches long on the top. Lani must have put some wax or something on there, it's sort of angled up to one side a bit. Seriously, it looks *amazing*. If I wasn't me,

I'd one hundred per cent think I was cool.

I end up staying for dinner at Kalia's. Her mum and dad both got home at about five and by half past we're sat round the table eating this amazing stew with sticky rice. Kalia's other brother, Noa, comes in halfway through dinner with his girlfriend, but it's not a problem; they just cook up some more rice and add a few more vegetables to the stew. Nothing here *ever* seems to be a problem.

'So where do you live, Will?' asks Kalia's mum.

Ordinarily I find this question kind of tricky. See, everyone knows Cherry Orchards and what it's like there, but you know what? For some reason tonight I just don't care.

'That'll be Cherry Orchards,' I say once I've finished my mouthful.

'*Right* . . .' says Kalia's dad slowly.

Like I say, everyone round here knows that place.

'We've been there a little while now,' I continue, 'while my dad's getting better.'

'What's up with your dad?' asks Kalia.

'He had an accident at work,' I say. 'It's been pretty bad actually; he could barely walk for a while, so I have to help out quite a bit, you know?'

'Sounds rough,' she says.

I nod. I *actually* nod for some reason. What's the point in pretending it's not? 'Yeah,' I reply, 'it is. He just can't get a break. You know? Every job he goes for ends up going to someone else.'

Kalia's dad looks over at me. 'You know, when I first moved to London, I slept in a car for two months while I saved up for a rental deposit. And, while it was a bad time, it eventually brought me everything that was good in my life. If it hadn't been for *that* moment, I wouldn't have met your mum.'

'Come off it, Dad!' interrupts Kalia. 'You've told us this story *SO* many times! Look, not *everyone* needs to sleep in a car to make things better!' She turns to me. 'Sorry, Will, Dad just *loves* to get all mystical about the universe bringing what you need when you need it most.'

Her father laughs. 'All right, Kalia,' he says, holding his

hands up in mock defeat. 'Look, I'm not saying *that*! What I *am* saying is that it was a bad time, right? And that *now* things are different. Things are *good*.' He gestures round at the room, at his family, at me. 'You know, Will, life is *always* changing, and you never know what's round the corner.'

Usually if someone said something like that to me, my brain would be all like, *Yes, I know that life is always changing – I used to live in a nice house with both my parents and now I'm in a tiny freezing-cold flat with my dad who can't work because of his terrible leg injuries.* But for some reason, here in their flat, where everything feels light and comfortable, that's *not* how I'm feeling. Instead, I'm imagining what it must have been like for him back then – a young man, moving to a brand-new country where he thought everything was going to be amazing and then having to live in a car for two months.

'That can't have been much fun,' I say.

Kalia slaps her forehead in an exaggerated way. 'Don't *encourage* him!'

'It was winter too . . .' adds Kalia's dad. '*Very* cold. Certainly a *lot* colder than I was used to.'

'*See!*' exclaims Kalia. 'He just can't help himself! You know what's coming next, don't you? The bit where Mum sees him in there early one morning and brings him a blanket!'

'Well, *that's* what happened!' protests Kalia's dad but he's smiling; they're all smiling.

'Then she looks at him . . .' adds Noa.

'And he looks at her . . .' continues Kalia.

'And we both fell in *loooooooooooove!*' joins in Kalia's mum, rubbing her husband's shoulder and grinning at him.

And it's all just *so* nice, *so* warm – I feel like somewhere along the line I must have fallen through the ice into a freezing river and it's only *now* that I'm finally sitting down by a fire. I can practically feel myself steaming.

Kalia's dad glances over towards me. 'Look, Will . . . I know that life can be hard. I understand, yes? So any time you want to come round here for dinner or anything, you feel free. *Okay?*'

I feel a huge sudden rush of gratitude, not just for that offer but for everything tonight. For letting me feel normal for a couple of hours. My eyes sting and I have to breathe slowly and bite my lip to keep everything under control, then I manage to nod and say, 'Thanks.'

And then, after we've all helped wash up and put away the dishes, that's it. I'm stood outside Kalia's flat and she's leaning against the doorway.

'See you tomorrow then?' she says.

'*Absolutely*,' I say.

My cheeks feel hot and my pulse throbs in my ears. That sounded, you know . . . a bit keen. I didn't mean it like *that* . . . But Kalia doesn't notice, or if she does notice, she doesn't make anything of it. She just grins as she waves and turns back in to her flat.

I press play on the Walkman, walk up the concrete steps and towards home, feeling the sharp chill of the evening air against my ears and the side of my head. And yeah, it's pretty cold, but even if I had it with me, there's no *way* I'd put that hat back on – not with my hair looking *this* good.

The music throbs in my ears and I grin, walking in time to the music, enjoying the car lights as they glide past. Everything seems to be happening at exactly the right time with the music. A bus speeds up past me just as the song swells to the chorus and then a bunch of joggers sprint past, light beams from their head torches bouncing around in time to the beat.

I laugh to myself. I love it when everything's like that – when it all just feels *right*. I'd almost forgotten the feeling. You know, *actual* happiness? I feel light, almost floating, like there's no problem that can't be solved. And, I tell you what, tomorrow I am sorting things out with Cameron. No matter what. No excuses, no delays. I walk a bit quicker, a rush of excitement tingling through me, bursting to get out. I speed up even more, eventually breaking into a run, going as fast as I can. Grinning wildly as the cold air rushes towards me, I run until my breath's hot and raw in my throat, until my legs start to

ache and then I keep on running.

After a while I notice a shadow gliding along on the ground nearby. It's broad and fast, weaving a bit from side to side. I shoot a look upwards and *almost* catch a glimpse of something large and pale with flapping broad silvery wings, as it sweeps round the corner of a building, up in front of the moon and away into the open night sky.

CHAPTER TWENTY

THE NEXT DAY, I WAKE UP FEELING,
well . . . you know, *good*. And maybe that's all it takes?
Just a bit of life – *real* life. A few nice moments with
people who might actually care one way or another what
happens to you – moments that actually *mean* something.

So, yeah . . . I'm walking towards school feeling all
pumped up and optimistic. It's weird, I even feel like I'm
walking differently, not shuffling like normal, but kind
of striding. My head's held up and I'm actually looking
around. Then I hear my name shouted out. I glance round.

Chris Tucker is stood on the corner of the road nearby.

'Looking sharp, mate!' he says.

I pause, waiting for the punchline, but there isn't one. He just nods approvingly. 'D'you get it done at the Turkish place?' he asks, inspecting my haircut. 'That's a tight fade!'

'A friend did it,' I reply.

'If any of *my* friends tried to cut my hair, I'd end up looking like I put my head in a blender!' he says with a grin.

'To be fair, that's how it looked after I tried,' I say, smiling.

I'm *smiling*? What the hell's going on?

Chris laughs. 'Right . . . Is that why you had that hat on the other day, when you'd been at your mum's?'

I nod. This is weird. This is all SO weird.

'So what's it like round at your mum's?' asks Chris. 'Better than Cherry Orchards, I'll bet?'

He says *Cherry Orchards* as though he's some old-fashioned TV presenter.

195

'Where *isn't*?' I say.

'Fair point . . .' He nods. 'So what are your folks like? Are they cool?'

'*Cool*?'

'Yeah, you know? Can you get away with stuff?' He grins. 'My mum's cool, see? My brother gave me these cans of cider at the weekend and she found them in my room, but didn't say *anything*! Not a peep – pretty sweet, right?'

'Pretty sweet,' I say, thinking that *actually* it sounded kind of messed up.

'So what's your dad like?' I ask.

Chris shrugs. 'Dunno, haven't seen him in years.'

'That's rough,' I say.

Chris gestures dismissively. 'Don't bother me. He's a waste of space. Better off without him. See, he thought he was something *once*, but he's just some soft old loser now – you know what I mean?'

'*Right* . . .' I say. 'Yeah.' Although actually I've got no idea what he means at all.

'So you skipped out on school yesterday?' says Chris. '*Cool.*'

It's my turn to shrug. 'It wasn't like that,' I say. 'I just needed to NOT be there. You know?'

'Tell me about it!' he says, grinning. 'I feel like that most days. Total waste of time, right?'

'Yeah . . .' I say again, not sure how else to respond.

'Anyway, I've got something to do,' says Chris suddenly as we're walking past the newsagent's, 'need to pick something up for a mate of mine. See you later, Will.'

'Yeah, later then, Chris,' I reply as I carry on walking, shaking my head slowly from side to side.

As it turns out, school was fine. Like, totally fine. *Better* than fine. Kalia's mum had phoned the office and explained *everything* to the head of Pastoral. So instead of a detention and a whole bunch of long conversations, I find myself having Mr Fraser sort of apologise for how things went down yesterday. I mean, it wasn't like an *apology* apology – that's not really his style, and he did make it totally clear that I was *never* to just up and leave school again – but I do think he genuinely felt bad that his lesson had turned into a *Let's All Rip It Out of Will* session. So, yeah, he's kind of gone into my good books a bit. He's definitely out of my BAD books anyway.

Kalia was right too. Some kid in Year Eleven got suspended today for setting fire to a bin in the science labs and setting off all the sprinklers, meaning that his whole class *and* the teacher got soaked. So that filled up most of the chat around school, and nobody was all that interested in the whole Will's-hat thing.

Besides, now that I've got this new haircut, I've noticed that people look at me a bit differently, you know? They do this little double take to check that it's me. A couple of kids even said that it looked decent. So, yeah, nice one, Lani!

In fact, the only bad thing about today was that I didn't see Cameron *or* Kalia. Cameron was off sick or something, and Kalia I just didn't see because she's not in my year. I mean, over lunchtime I did try to hang out in some places that I thought she might be, but that felt a bit weird and pushy so I stopped doing that and just got on with my day.

Still, hopefully my phone'll be working again once I open the rice box and I can get her details or something?

Anyway, that was my day. Pretty great, all in all, and I'm still in a good mood all the way home. Right up until I open the door. And as soon as I do that I know something's wrong.

It's weird. There's just this thick heavy atmosphere, you know? Like, I can actually *feel* it, like the air's made of tar.

'Hey, Dad,' I call out, 'you all right?'

I can see him. He's on the sofa but he doesn't say anything at first, doesn't even look in my direction. I feel this whooshing sensation as the room slides away from me and suddenly it's like all the joy's been sucked out of the world.

Something's happened. Something bad.

'Dad?' I rush through to the room. 'Are you okay?'

He looks round at me. His face blank, a mask. 'Didn't

get the job . . .' he says, his voice flat as he limply holds up a letter.

I knew it. I just *knew* it.

'That's all right,' I say, leaning over and putting my hand on his shoulder. 'Come on! There'll be other jobs, right?'

'Sure,' he mumbles, the word falling from his mouth like a stone. He doesn't say anything else.

'Look, don't worry about it!' I say. 'That just wasn't the right job for you.'

'But *none* of them are!' he says. 'I don't know what to do, Will. I've tried *everything*, but nothing works.' He looks up at me with awful empty eyes. 'I'm tired.'

'Look, we'll work something out!' I say, the same upbeat, optimistic, totally fake voice that wouldn't convince a six-year-old. 'We always do, right?'

'Right,' he mutters, then slowly closes his eyes. 'Look . . . I'm going to bed, Will. I'm just tired – *really* tired.'

'Okay,' I reply, not mentioning that it's only five p.m., doing everything I can to ignore how wrong this all feels. 'Well, see you in the morning then, Dad,' I add, as he heaves himself up and limps slowly towards the door. I watch him go, hoping that he'll turn and do that stupid goofy hopeful smile of his.

He doesn't.

So, yeah, I know that things are bad. I mean, *obviously*. But I didn't realise quite *how* bad it was until I get woken up in the middle of the night.

Cold air pinches at me and my breath swirls out, a cloud of mist illuminated by the glow of the street lights gleaming in through the thin curtains.

My heart jolts. An awful noise is coming from the room next to mine – a gulping, gasping, retching sound. *What is it?*

My pulse thuds through my chest, up into my throat and ears, pounding hard but not loud enough to drown out that dreadful sound. Then it stops, collapsing into broken sobs and I recognise what it is.

It's crying.

It's my dad, crying.

ACT
THREE

CHAPTER TWENTY-ONE

I WAKE UP LATE AND HURRY downstairs. Usually Dad would be sat there looking at me with an eyebrow raised, saying something like, *Oh! You've finally decided to join us then?* and then I'd say something like, *Well, you know, Dad, I need to get my beauty sleep.* And then he'd push a cup of tea over, we'd have breakfast together and I'd leave for school while he set off to do the rounds of all the agencies to see if there's anything new that he can apply for.

Not today, though. There's no sign of him, and he's

clearly not already up. There's no mug on the draining rack and the kettle's stone cold. I think about waking him but decide not to – if *I* had a bad night, then *his* must have been even worse.

An oppressive force pushes in at me from the bare walls. I mean, our flat never feels like a big place, but right now it feels unbearably small. I've not had anything to eat yet, but if I mix up some oats with water and put it in the microwave, that just means spending more time here, which right now I'm keen to avoid. Besides, I'm probably going to be late anyway, so I just grab a hoody and leave.

I'm thinking about everything and nothing while I walk – totally absorbed in my own thoughts and walking on autopilot, so I barely even hear my name being called out and footsteps hurrying up behind me.

'Didn't you see me?' asks Cameron, slightly out of breath, his face flushed. 'I've been waving at you like an idiot since I saw you from the end of my road.'

I smile as I turn to look at him – good old Cameron.

'Sorry, mate, I was miles away.'

'Weird . . . It *looks* like you're right there!' he says, reaching out and prodding me with one finger.

'Oh yeah! So I am!' I reply, looking around and pretending to be surprised.

Cameron grins. 'Nice haircut by the way,' he adds. 'Definitely an improvement . . .'

I snort out a laugh. 'Cheers. Kalia's brother did it.'

'*Kalia's* brother?'

'Yeah, I went round to hers the other night.'

'Sorry. *What?* You went round to *her* house? Kalia's house? Are we talking about the same Kalia here? Like, *Kalia-I-Take-No-Crap-From-Anyone?*'

'That'd be the one. Do you know any other Kalias?'

Cameron whistles under his breath. 'Hanging out with the cool kids now, eh? You're going to forget all about little old me.' He does these stupid puppy-dog eyes and I laugh, *properly* laugh.

'*As if!*' I reply. 'You can't have W/C Games without both a W and a C!'

'There you go!' he says, punching me on the arm, then he puts on a terrible version of the accent that Gru guy does in those *Despicable Me* films. 'Now *that's* what I'm talking about!' He grins at me and I grin back.

It's weird; despite what happened last night I'm suddenly feeling a bit better. You know when you're feeling really low and you think what you need is to lock yourself away on your own, but what you *actually* need is to have one of your friends make you laugh by being an idiot?

Cameron pauses for a moment and puts his hand on my shoulder. 'And, Will, look – I'm sorry, you know, for . . . well, you know.'

I wave my hand. 'Mate, don't worry about it. I'm sorry too. I totally overreacted –' I glance over at him but suddenly feel a bit weird, so I look down at the ground – 'and when I heard about your trainers . . .' I breathe in through my teeth. '*Nightmare.*

I bet your folks completely *lost* it!'

Cameron shakes his head and rubs at the back of his neck. 'Tell me about it! The *worst* part is that when I left for school that day, Mum said, "Are you *sure* it's a good idea to take them into school? They *did* cost a lot of money," and I said, "Come on, Mum, relax! They'll be on my feet or in my locker – it'll be fine!"' He pauses and looks at me. 'Shows what I know, *right*?'

'How were *you* to know your locker would get smashed open?'

He shrugs. 'Yeah, maybe. I dunno . . . It made me think, though. Like, perhaps they were a bit, you know . . . a bit *much*?'

'*No*,' I say sharply, surprising myself, 'you're *wrong*. Look, if someone else can't cope because *you've* got something nice and they want to take it or spoil it or whatever, then that's *their* problem, not yours. *Okay*?' I look him directly in the eyes. 'You've got *nothing* to feel bad about.'

'Whoa!' says Cameron, holding his hands up,

pretending to step back warily. 'Now *that* was intense!'

I laugh again. 'A bit much?'

Cameron grins and holds out his thumb and forefinger as though measuring something. 'Just a *teeeeny* bit!'

I pat him on the back. 'Look, Cameron, sure you've got some nice stuff, but it's not like you're ever rubbing anyone's face in it. And, let's face it, if anyone's going to know if you *were*, it would be me. Right?'

'Cheers, Will,' he says, glancing over at me. He pauses for a second. 'So we're good?'

'We're good.'

Cameron's smile's so big that his face near enough splits in two, and he pulls this big exaggerated expression of relief. 'Mate, I can't tell you *how* happy I am to hear that – if I had to sit next to Elsie Woodleigh in any more lessons, I think I'd end up eating my own ears!'

'Yeah, she *does* like a bit of a chat, doesn't she?'

Cameron just looks at me, totally deadpan, until I start laughing, then *he* starts laughing, and then he sort of stumbles and accidentally drops his bag and for some reason *that* is the funniest thing in the world and now we're both bent double, laughing so hard that tears are rolling down my cheeks and the dense waves of darkness that have been pushing in at me recently feel like they're receding a bit.

CHAPTER TWENTY-TWO

IT'S GREAT THAT WE WERE ABLE to have that chat because today's one of those days that I don't share any lessons with Cameron and he has clubs all lunchtime, so if we'd not sorted things out then, I don't know when we would have.

So, yeah, I know I look like a bit of a Billy One-Mate going into the canteen on my own, but I don't mind because *I* know that's not true. I'm definitely Billy *One*-Mates, maybe even Billy *Two*-Mates if you count Kalia? I mean, I *definitely* count Kalia, but I'm not sure if she'd count me yet.

All the same, I won't lie, I did look around the hall to see if she was in there and was kind of gutted that she wasn't. But still, it's lunchtime and I didn't have any breakfast so I'm properly hungry now.

It's an easy choice once I get to the front of the queue – mac and cheese, no contest! Dad's always reminding me to get as much as I can for lunch, since it's the one meal of the day that's free. And to make things even better, it's Sam dishing up today. He used to work in that cafe where I drew those pictures on the walls – so I've known him for years.

He grins at me as I slide my tray along the rails towards him. 'All right, chief?' he says. 'All good with you?'

'Good enough, Sam!' I reply, then pause. '*Actually* . . . better than good! I sorted something out with a mate earlier. We'd had a row, but it's all fixed now.'

'Good for you!' says Sam, nodding. 'No point letting these things fester!'

He's one hundred per cent right there. 'And how're you?'

He grins and spreads his hands wide. 'You know me,

Will – living my best life!'

If he'd been anyone else, that might have seemed sarcastic, but that's not Sam's way – he always seems genuinely happy. Mum told me that he used to live on the streets or something, so I guess he's been through a lot. But whatever the reason, that's just his thing – every day's a new day. Tell you what, respect where it's due. I wish *I* had that attitude.

'So what's it going to be then?' asks Sam.

'Got to be the mac and cheese, right?'

'An excellent choice, sir!' says Sam, putting on a posh waiter's voice as he puts a MASSIVE portion on the plate *and* it's a corner piece with all the crispy bits – *sweet*! He loads up all the chopped tomatoes, cucumber and salad too.

'Got to have your greens!' he says. 'Balanced diet and all that!'

'Cheers, Sam!' I reply, and then that's it.

I mean, it doesn't sound like much, but it's another one of those things that just makes me feel better. I know that probably sounds daft, like it shouldn't really mean *anything*, but when you've hardly got anything, it doesn't take a whole lot to turn things round – and a nice little chat and a double-size portion of mac and cheese will *definitely* help.

I'm looking around for somewhere to sit when I hear someone call my name. Now, you'll probably have guessed by now that this isn't exactly an everyday occurrence. I was hoping that I'd just find an empty table and sit there, but instead it's only Chris Tucker, gesturing to a seat next to him, while his mates look on with golf-ball eyes.

'Will? Hey, *Will*! Over here, mate!'

Seriously, what is actually happening? I mean, I'm not the only one to think that. I can see it on everyone's faces. It's not that anyone *says* anything or even looks round, but I feel the weight of people just, you know . . . noticing.

Chris beckons me over. For a moment longer I just stand there, weighing something up in my mind – but I'm not sure exactly what. Then I shrug and walk over to his table.

Chris shoves out the chair next to him with his leg and using his pretend-posh-TV-presenter voice says, 'Take a seat.'

I do.

Zayn looks sideways at me, like he can smell something bad, then he glances over at Chris, but Chris is only looking at me.

'You all right then, Will?' he asks.

'Yeah, good,' I reply.

'Hey, did you lot hear that Will went AWOL the other

day?' asks Chris, looking round at the group. A few of the other kids nod or sort of shrug, clearly uncertain of what the correct response should be. Chris is going totally off script here. I mean, the fact that he's not flipped my dinner tray or tried to trip me up is weird enough, but now he's also talking to me like we're friends and, to be honest, nobody quite knows what to make of that. Me included.

'Yeah, he's a *nutter* this one!' says Chris. 'A bit of a dark horse.'

'A bit of a donkey, more like,' says Zayn. Then he looks at Chris. 'Come on, mate, are you joking? What's Poundland doing over here?'

Chris's expression darkens and he looks over at Zayn for less than a second. 'Leave it out, Z,' he says. 'Will's all right, *yeah*?'

And apparently that's all it takes. The other kids in the group kind of raise their eyebrows but nobody says anything. They certainly don't say anything bad about me. Neither does Zayn. But he looks at me like he's thinking bad things about me. Very bad things.

Tell you what, life's weird. It just feels like I *never* know what's coming. And, of course, like Kalia's dad says, *no one* does, but I reckon I could go for a *bit* more certainty all the same. I feel like there's this big red RANDOMISER button hidden in my life somewhere and *someone* keeps slamming their hand down on it. If you look at my life when I was a young kid, it was all fine. Sure, we didn't have a massive house or go on fancy holidays or anything, but we were okay – we had all the bases covered. Then boom! RANDOMISER! Mum leaves and I need to get used to just living with Dad. Not long after that: RANDOMISER! Dad loses his job. Then: RANDOMISER! We have to move to Cherry Orchards. RANDOMISER! Dad gets injured. RANDOMISER! I start at high school and *everything* gets thrown up in the air again.

And now . . . RANDOMISER! It looks like I might even be friends with Chris Tucker. The kid who's basically bullied me since he first saw me.

Still, I guess that makes me Billy Three-Mates?

CHAPTER TWENTY-THREE

ACTUALLY . . . YOU KNOW WHAT?
I was wrong about the whole randomiser thing. Life's *not* random – it's a roller coaster. If you ever find yourself going up, then you'd better get ready for the drop – because *that's* what's coming next.

So I'm walking home, all happy, you know? I mean, Mr Prince really rates that owl I painted, I've made up with Cameron, and *now* it's looking like I've also got two new friends as well. I know it's not like I've just won the lottery or anything, but life feels okay.

I look up as I'm walking out of the underpass into Cherry Orchards, and you'll never guess what. There's this bright beam of light shining down through a break in the clouds. Talk about symbolism. I grin. Dad's going to love it when I tell him that – he's a sucker for any sort of 'sign'.

Like I said, life feels good. And it's *still* feeling good all the way up the staircase, even though it smells like all the local cats think it's their toilet. I'm taking the steps two at a time, kind of jogging up them. See, I reckon that I know what I can do to pull Dad out of his mood.

Now that I'm feeling better, it's like I can see a few options that just didn't seem to be there before. You know, I can help him out a bit with the handyman stuff evenings and weekends – many hands make light work and all that. We could finish the jobs quicker, get more money in. You never know, we could even set up a little business or something? I mean, it might not bring in *loads* of money, but like the guy in the shop by my mum's said, every little helps, right?

So that's how I'm feeling all the way along the balcony

until I turn the corner and see someone standing at our door – a broad back leaning heavily against the wall – and *that's* when everything drops . . .

It's Damien Forsyth.

I just stand totally still for a moment. Sickness floods through me. My hands are literally shaking, as I try to convince my jelly legs to do what I want them to.

It's hard to say how old Damien is. I mean, I know he's not *young*, but you couldn't put a concrete age to him. He's not like one of the lads on the estate, trying to prove themselves, trying to make a name. He's already done all that and more. His face is drawn with cruel hard lines. It's a face that tells a story, and not a nice one. He tilts his head from one side to the other, gently massaging his thick neck.

'Listen, Pinky,' says Damien, talking to my dad, 'you *knew* the deal . . . I'm not running a charity here.' He speaks with no expression at all. His deep voice sounding like a speaker that's blown, almost distorted. I've never been close enough to him to hear his voice before. And

I'll tell you what, I'll be happy if it *never* happens again.

'I know, Damien,' says my dad, 'and I'm sorry about the delay. I really am. I just need a bit more time. *Please?*'

The tone in his voice, the desperation, is almost too much to bear. I mean, how have we got *here*?

Damien looks at Dad for a while and then shrugs. 'Thing is, you've got to pay back your debts –' his voice vibrates along the balcony floor to me – 'otherwise the people that are owed money get nervous. You know? They start to worry. What if their money's not actually coming back? They might have to make some *difficult* decisions. Do things they might not want to have to. Just to make sure they get the money back. Just so nobody thinks they're going soft.' He pauses again and leans in closer, locking eyes with my dad. 'You understand me?'

Dad nods.

Damien holds his gaze for a long couple of seconds. 'Good,' he says, then he turns to face me. 'You Pinky's boy?'

'Yeah . . .' I reply, my voice pulled as tight as a guitar string.

'Must be tough,' Damien says, 'him not working and all.'

I nod.

'People round here want to help, though,' adds Damien. 'I offered him a job just now. Easy money. Just to help make sure he could repay his debts.' Damien looks at me with those blank lifeless eyes. 'He turned me down.' He shakes his head, looking almost amused. 'Said that he had some money coming in. I mean, personally I don't care where the money comes from . . . as long as I get it. *Right?*'

I shoot a look at my dad's face – a horrible sickly pallid sheen is washing over him – it's impossible to tell what he's thinking in that moment. 'Yeah,' I say, my dry throat catching on every word, 'we've got something coming up.'

Damien looks at me for a couple of seconds, deep in the eyes, and then he nods. 'Well, that *is* good news.'

I nod. I couldn't speak now, even if I wanted to.

'*Right!*' Damien claps his hands briskly together, a sudden sharp sound that ricochets off the walls. 'Best be off. You know, things to do. See you soon, Pinky. Forty-eight hours. *All right?*'

He nods at me, then turns and walks along the balcony, his broad shoulders blocking out what little light is left.

Now there are no beams of light shining down through the clouds. Now everything is heavy and grey.

Now I know we're *really* in trouble.

CHAPTER TWENTY-FOUR

I PUSH PAST DAD, STORMING INTO the flat. It's freezing in here – of *course* it is. Dad's all wrapped up in a scarf and three jumpers.

'Are you all right, Will?' he asks. 'Look, I'm sorry about . . . *that*. About all of it.'

I just look at him.

'Come on, Will!' he says, his voice rising in pitch. 'Talk to me. *Please.*'

But I don't say anything. *What is there to say?*

I stand there a while in the freezing silence and I don't

know whether to scream, cry or smash everything I can see.

'Look. It's all going to be okay. All we need to—' starts Dad, but I interrupt.

'All we need to do is *what*?' I ask. The bitterness in my voice makes my mouth sting. '*What on earth* can we *possibly* do that we haven't been doing already? Because I don't know if you've noticed, but things haven't been going SO great this last couple of years.' I glare at him and his eyes widen. I don't think I've ever spoken to him like this. I don't know why I am right now.

He looks at me with these soft hurt eyes, but something's switched inside me. Something dangerous, and it's like the floodgates have been opened – there's no stopping it.

'You know what they say that Damien does to people who don't pay him? I don't know if you've heard any of the stories? But *I* have.'

Dad looks away.

I nod. 'Yeah, that's right – you get to hear *lots* of nice things like that living round here.'

'Look, I'm sorry!' says Dad. 'I messed up by borrowing off him. I *know* I did, but I'll get it all sorted out – I *promise*. I've got a couple of things lined up.'

'Yeah? Well, that's *lovely* . . .' I reply, 'but promises aren't going to work for Damien! He wants *money.*' I just look at him, shaking my head. 'Which we don't have. What were you *thinking*? I mean, *seriously*! That guy is really scary!'

Dad slumps back on the sofa, looking smaller, older and thinner than he did even a second or two before. And I know that I should try to make things better here. I know I could pat him on the shoulder, hug him even, tell him that we're both on the same team and that as long as we're together we'll be okay. But I don't do any of those things. I can't – I'm too angry.

'I'm *sorry* . . .' Dad repeats, barely looking at me.

I stare at him for a moment and somehow my reply just happens.

'*You should be,*' I say, the words spilling out like poison. Then I turn round and walk straight back out of the flat.

A bitter wind billows down the dark streets, making my hands tight and stiff. I've only got a hoody on over my school shirt and it's nowhere near enough. I feel like I might as well be wearing nothing. Every inch of me feels cold, almost numb. I'm not even crying now. I'm past that. What's the point?

Even so, I can't help myself. I keep looking out for something *good*, something to lift my mood, but there's *nothing*. I keep half an eye up towards the sky, hoping for a flash of silver, a white blur, something to suggest that the whole world's not rotten to core. But there's nothing there.

When I get in, it's late. There's a note from Dad but I ignore it. Seriously, I'm past caring. What can it *possibly* say that can make any of this better?

I kick off my stupid shoes and fall into bed fully clothed.

Tomorrow's another day, right? I mean, sure . . . people say that, but *realistically*? What's going to be different? *Nothing*. Chances are that tomorrow's going to be just as bad as today.

CHAPTER TWENTY-FIVE

I *FALL ASLEEP QUICKLY, BUT THEN* in the middle of the night I wake up and it's like something has been turned on in my brain. A tap that's spitting out bad thoughts. I want to run away but I can't, because you can't run from your own mind. Needless to say, I don't get much sleep after that.

I crawl out of bed for school in the morning, feeling like I'm walking through a dream – everything's drifting and unreal. Peering in the mirror I almost laugh.

'What a *mess!*' I mutter. My eyes are sunken, with

greenish grey smudges underneath. My cheeks look hollow and drawn – I look awful.

I go downstairs to fix something for breakfast, feeling all jittery and weird. To be honest, I'm worried about seeing Dad. I mean, I'm still angry with him. Not in the same way – it's not that frightening HOT anger any more – but I don't feel anywhere near 'right', so God knows what I'm likely to say. I peer round the door into the kitchen because I really can't face seeing him, but, as it happens, the kitchen's empty. He's already gone out and left another note for me.

Hey Will,

I've got a few things lined up today. It'll all come good. I swear it will! We've just got to hang in there, okay? We can get through this. I'll make it right, I promise.

Have a good day at school.

see you later,

D X

Yeah, *whatever.*

We still have a few cornflakes left so I pour them into a bowl. It's not till then that I realise we've no UHT left. So I make up the last of the lemon squash from the cupboard and pour that over instead. You know what? Don't knock it till you've tried it. Then, *after* you've tried it, you can knock it all you like. It's pretty horrible.

Anyway, off to school . . . I feel so wired that I don't want to see *anyone*. Not Kalia, not Cameron, no one. On the walk in there's this guy in front of me on the bit of pavement where it goes really narrow by the road down by the railway bridge and he's walking really slowly and talking on his phone, laughing like an idiot and occasionally saying, 'Nice one, Stubbsy,' and it's making me want to grab his phone off him and smash it into tiny pieces, then scream at him to get the hell out of my way. So *that's* the frame of mind I'm in. And, yeah, I'm not proud of myself, but that's just how I feel. I guess that's what hunger and sleep deprivation do for you.

Once I get into school, I just keep my head down, ignoring anyone and everyone. I do the bare minimum to get through the lessons and *not* get told off – I don't want to have to talk to any teachers either.

I sort of sleepwalk through the whole day without saying a single word to anyone apart from 'here' in registration, which in a way *almost* feels like an achievement. Maybe the head will do a shout-out in assembly for me tomorrow? Most time wasted in a school day?

The last lesson of the day is Art, which puts me in a slightly better mood. By the time I'm walking in through the art-room doors, I *don't* feel like I hate the whole world and everyone in it.

Mr Prince isn't there, though. It's Mr Morrison instead, who the school *always* gets in for cover, and my heart sinks. *Everyone* gives him a hard time, which means that the room's going to be all hectic, and that's the *last* thing I need today.

'Right then,' says Mr Morrison, his voice thin and reedy. 'Settle down, please.'

There is no settling down.

'Come on *now* –' his voice sounding more nasally the louder it gets – 'I know it's the last period of the day and you're all tired, but would you *please* settle down?'

Again there is no settling down.

This pattern carries on for another five minutes or so

until Mr Morrison says that if this continues, he'll have to get the deputy head.

I shake my head. *That* was a bad move. He's as good as admitted he's got no control. Now the whole lesson's out the window. There's another five minutes or so of chaos and then the deputy head Mrs Fairweather is called in to sort everything out.

She stands there, looking all formidable until everyone shuts up, then she tells us how disappointed in us all she is.

Then Amba says that not *everyone* was acting up, and Mrs Fairweather replies that it doesn't matter if it wasn't *everyone*, if she's had to stop what she's doing to come down to a classroom to remind students how to behave, then it's totally unacceptable whether it was five students or fifteen who were misbehaving.

It's all *so* predictable.

Anyway, by the time the room's quiet the lesson's nearly halfway over.

'As you all know,' says Mr Morrison, 'the deadline for

the wildlife art competition is today, so make sure you have your entries submitted by the end of the day.'

There's a buzz of conversation at this, but my heart sinks. I'd forgotten all about it and my phone's *still* in its rice prison back at Mum's house. When Mr Morrison's finished trying to talk to the class, I walk over to him.

'Sir, Mr Prince told me that he'd help me photograph my painting with the school cameras and lights. Do you know where they are and how to use them?'

'Do I *look* like I would know that?' says Mr Morrison, scowling as he looks around the room, barely even glancing over at me before he points over to Sharine and Alex who have both got their phones out and says, '*Excuse me!*' in a loud but ineffective voice.

No, I think to myself, *you look like you couldn't cook a Pot Noodle*. But I don't say that. I just walk away and go back to my desk, with the owl painting set neatly out in front of me.

Well, that's that then. There's no one here whose phone I can borrow to take a photo of my painting. At least no one that I *want* to ask – certainly not today. I'm just *so* tired. Tired of everything. My brain's itching, but I can't get to the itch. You know? It's just this feeling of wrongness inside me, and it's *constant*.

It's not long before everyone's messing about again. I can just about hear Mr Morrison trying to get them all back under control but the sound seems to come from miles away, deep   underwater.

Two lads are literally throwing powder paint at each other in billowing clouds of colour. I take a deep breath, trying to sort my head out, but I feel like I'm on some stupid fairground ride that just won't stop.

I look at my painting again, trying to focus on something, trying to calm my mind. But the painting seems empty now, drained of all life. It's not this vibrant wild creature; it's just a few sloppy marks on a piece of paper. Total rubbish. What was Mr Prince on about? There's no way it could win anything. It's *stupid* and so am I.

The whole room's vibrating. It's like that part in a track where it's all rising, rising, *rising* and you're waiting for the beat to kick in. Everyone's shrieking, laughing, running around, but nothing's making any sense – I can't understand any words. It's all just garbled sounds bouncing round the room and colliding into each other.

I can't cope. I mean, it's one thing having the chaos sloshing around *inside* your brain, but when it starts spilling out into the world around you, it all feels a bit much, you know? I try to keep calm and ride it out, but all of a sudden I feel trapped. I need to get out. Fire burns up through me. There's no point in *anything*.

My hands grip the desk, my knuckles bleached to a sickly yellow white with threads of blood-red shot through.

I'm vaguely aware of ripping the painting into pieces, screwing it all up and throwing it across the room. I see Omari watching me, his eyes wide. His mouth moves up and down but I can't make out any of his words so I just ignore him. Standing up on trembling legs, I stumble through to the back of the room, where all the sinks are.

That awful garbled noise is still happening so I stand there a moment, staring into the darkness of the plughole, trying to ignore it. But that doesn't help. Moving automatically, I swing open the double doors that lead out on to the patio. And I leave.

I'm sure that people notice, but perhaps they don't. I don't know. I don't care.

I don't care about *anything*.

There's this tree round the back of the art block, I'm not sure what sort. It's got big leaves but it's definitely not a conker tree, which is pretty much the only tree I know. Anyway, it's somewhere that I like to sit when the weather's nice. I mean, it's *not* nice today, but I sit there anyway.

Over time, the weird feeling wears off, and the blood stops throbbing in my ears and washes away, leaving me feeling cold, blank and wiped out. The minutes roll by and then I hear the bell for the end of the day. I sit there a bit longer, waiting for the scrum in the cloakroom to be over, then I go to get my stuff and walk home.

As I leave through the gates, I see Chris, Zayn and that lot over by the gates.

Chris shouts over. 'All right, Will? You want to head into town with us?'

'Sure,' I reply, my voice totally empty. 'Why not?'

'Today would be good!' he says, clapping his hands briskly together. 'Come on, *chop-chop*!'

I shoulder my bag and start to walk over when I feel a hand on my back.

I turn round; it's Cameron.

'Listen, Will,' he says in a quick low voice, 'you don't want to get mixed up with Chris. You *know* what he's like.'

'Right,' I say. 'And what *is* he like, Cameron?'

'You *know*!' insists Cameron. 'Come on, Will! I know things have been a bit weird with us recently, but *seriously*, those lads are bad news.' He shakes his head. 'Look, do you want to come back to mine? We can do a bit more work on our game, *right*?'

And yeah, on some level I *know* that he's right – I'm not stupid. And if it had been *any* other day and I had been feeling *any* other way, I'd have slapped him on the back, made some stupid joke about W/C Games and gone back to his. But it *is* today and I *am* feeling the way that I'm feeling.

The trouble is that *right now* the thought of going to Cameron's warm shiny house, with his warm shiny parents makes me feel like I wouldn't be able to breathe – like I'd be a fish out of water. *Literally.* At least with Chris there's nothing to make me feel bad. His life is just as messed up as mine – only in a different way.

So, yeah, I know what I *should* do – but I don't do it.

'Look, I'll see you later, Cameron, yeah?' I lightly shrug his hand off my shoulder and walk over to where Chris and the others are waiting.

I don't even look back. I mean, seriously . . . what's the point?

CHAPTER TWENTY-SIX

'**SO WHERE ARE WE GOING THEN?**'
I ask as we walk along Union Road, the long street that leads pretty much the whole way into town.

'You'll see,' mutters Zayn, finishing his last few crisps and letting the bag drop to the ground. 'But I don't know why *you're* here. We're probably going to get a drink on the way and *I'm* not subbing you!'

'Leave it out, Zayn,' says Chris. 'Will doesn't need *your* help. Who would?"

Everyone laughs apart from Zayn, whose jaw clenches

as he looks sharply away. While we're walking, Chris taps my arm and gestures for me to slow down. Once we're a bit behind everyone he starts talking in a low voice.

'Listen, I know you probably won't have any cash, but if you do me a favour, I can get you a fiver.'

'What sort of favour?' I ask.

'See, my headphones have had it,' he says. 'There's these headphones that I want, but they're *way* too much. Seriously, total rip-off! Cheaper in GameXchange, but still . . . more than I want to pay right now. You know?'

'Yeah,' I say. '*So* . . . what's the favour? You want to borrow mine?'

Chris snorts. 'No thanks, mate! I've got *some* pride!' Then he grins. 'Look, I'm just messing. I need them for gaming, so I need the headset ones, yeah? All you need to do is pick a pair up for me.'

'Just pick a pair up?'

'Sure,' he says, smiling like this is all totally fine. 'We just go in there and look about, waiting until there's only one person behind the desk. Then I'll ask about something from the lock-up, they open it up, I distract them and you pick up the headphones while they're not looking. *Easy.*'

'Come on, Chris!' I say, shaking my head. 'Stealing's not really my sort of thing, you know?'

'Fine,' he says, looking at me all casual. 'Zayn's going to *love* that!'

My heart's pounding, my mouth feels like it's sweating this nasty metallic taste. I shake my head, trying to stop myself from saying anything else, but somehow the words fall out of my mouth. 'And you'll do all the talking?' I say.

Chris's eyes light up. 'I *knew* you had it in you!' He slaps me on the back. 'Yeah, I'll deal with all the chat. Seriously. It'll be *easy* – I've done it before. You just look for my cue. *Right?* When it's time, I'll scratch my left eyebrow. Got it?'

Inside, I'm shaking my head, saying, *Thank you very much for asking, Chris, but no*, then turning round and walking to Cameron's house to lead my old, sensible life from before. But for *some* reason I find myself nodding and saying, 'Sounds easy enough.'

'Piece of cake,' replies Chris, grinning at me again. He shouts out to the rest of the group. 'Hey! Me and Will have just got to do something. Meet you at the station, right?'

Everyone nods or shouts 'sure' or 'see you in a bit', apart from Zayn who glares at me like he wants me to die horribly, or melt into the floor, or die horribly and *then* melt into the floor.

Chris and I turn on to the road that leads towards GameXchange and I walk silently in time with the pounding of my heartbeat, trying not to feel sick.

I've not been in GameXchange for years. I used to come in every now and then, sell a couple of old games and get a bit of money towards a new one, but since we sold the games console there's not really been much point.

It looks way nicer than it used to, though. Back then loads of dried leaves and rubbish used to blow in through the door. It was kind of grubby-looking and the people working here seemed like they'd rather be *anywhere* else. It's smarter now and there's this girl working in there with a ring through her lip and half her hair dyed blue.

She looks up as I walk in. 'You all right?' she asks, smiling.

I just nod and try to smile back. My throat feels tight – I'm sure my eyelid's twitching.

Just act normal.

Chris is over on the other side of the shop, totally ignoring me as we'd arranged. I put aside everything else and just try to stick to the plan. So I walk over to look at the budget games, round by the lock-up.

A minute or so passes and then Chris walks up to the counter. 'Excuse me,' he says, sounding different to how he usually speaks, 'have you got any of those headsets? You know, the VR ones?'

'Sure,' says the girl. 'Which one are you after?'

'I'm not sure,' says Chris. 'Which one do you think's the best?'

'It depends on what you want really,' she replies. 'Gaming, films, art stuff, socials?'

'I guess gaming mainly . . .' says Chris. 'I'm not sure. Can you talk me through the ones you've got?'

'Yeah, give me a second,' says the girl. She gets the keys out from behind the counter and slides the glass open past her. I'm stood directly behind her; the headphones are literally just an arm's reach away. Fair play to Chris, it's playing out *exactly* like he said it would.

As the girl takes out one of the headsets and hands it over to Chris, she starts talking about the various specs, all the pros and cons of the different systems.

'Yeah, I get you . . .' says Chris, looking right into her eyes and nodding as he lightly scratches his left eyebrow.

This is it. My hands are trembling. This really is *it*.

I'm sure that she'll turn round and ask why the room's shaking in time with the explosive thudding of my heartbeat, but she doesn't. She doesn't turn round as my arm slips into the lock-up and grabs the headphones. She doesn't even turn round as I slip the headphones into my open bag and turn back to the games rack, my vision blurred, my hands sweating.

I move down the aisle and look at a few more games for another minute or so – just like Chris told me to, trying to keep my breathing calm and regular. Then, as Chris keeps talking, I pick up my bag and walk to the door.

I've done it.

I've *actually* done it.

I'm halfway through the door when a voice calls out, '*Will?*'

I freeze, then slowly turn round, swallowing hard. I see Chris's eyes widen slightly, but apart from that he doesn't shift at all and just keeps chatting with the girl who's fiddling about with one of the headsets. Then I can see someone walking out through the door behind the counter. It's Kalia's older brother, Noa.

'I *thought* it was you!' he says. 'How you doing, mate?'

'Yeah, good,' I manage to croak out.

'So what you looking for then?' he asks, all light and

breezy. 'A new phone? Kalia told me that you'd fried your old one!'

'Nah, just some games,' I reply. 'I'm hoping my phone'll be all right. I've done the old rice trick.'

'Yeah, fingers crossed!' he says with a smile, then he catches sight of Chris and his brow furrows. 'You all right, Suzi?' Noa calls to the girl with the blue hair.

'Yeah, all good here!' she says. 'Just *dazzling* a customer with my specialist subject knowledge.'

Noa smiles. 'Yeah, for sure!' he replies. He's smiling, but he's clearly keeping an eye on Chris.

He turns briefly back to me., 'Well, I'd better get back to work,' he says. 'This place won't manage itself.'

'All right,' I say. 'See you around, Noa.'

'Yeah, see you later, Will!'

I raise a hand, then walk out of the shop on legs made of spaghetti.

Once I'm outside, I try to start breathing again. Noa's the manager of that shop. So I've just *stolen* from *him*.

I feel sick. Worse than sick. I feel ashamed. Everything's

a total mess. I walk off to the place that Chris and I had arranged to meet and sit on the bench, trying to push all the bad feelings away. Five minutes later, Chris comes along. He's swinging his arms as he walks, rolling his shoulders, walking down the pavement like he owns it.

'Mate!' he exclaims. 'That was EPIC. They had *no* idea. I mean, that manager guy was watching *me* like a hawk, but he had no idea that you'd already done the deed!'

He holds out his fist and we brush knuckles, but inside I feel terrible – like I've been filled up with burnt plastic, foam packaging and anything else bad that you can think of. I've just *stolen* from Noa. The other night round at Kalia's was the one time I've felt normal in ages and now I've just done *this?* To him? I can barely get in a whole breath.

'Pass them over then!' says Chris, holding his hand out. I reach into my bag, picking up the headphones but trying to touch them as little as possible. Even looking at them makes me feel sick.

'You were a machine in there!' says Chris. 'Wait till I tell

Zayn and the others!' His eyes light up, like he genuinely loves this, but the thought of *anyone* else knowing what I've done is just too much.

'You know what?' I mutter. 'I've got to go. I forgot about something I need to do for my dad. See you tomorrow, right?'

'Hey, *come on!*' He looks genuinely upset. 'What about the rest of the evening?' He fumbles about in his pocket. 'Look, at least let me give you that fiver? Fair's fair! You did me a solid back there!'

'Don't worry about it,' I call over my shoulder, my voice unsteady in my throat. '*Seriously.*'

'Fair enough,' says Chris. 'Have it your way!'

Then I'm walking away and I feel free. Immediately I put my own headphones on. Turning my back on Chris and every other *stupid* thing that's happened today.

I can feel tears rolling down my cheeks, freezing cold in the evening breeze, but I do nothing to brush them away. I feel terrible, but I deserve it – I *deserve* to feel this bad.

When I feel an arm round my shoulder, I nearly jump a mile, expecting it to be Noa – expecting to see anger and disappointment written all over his face. But it's not Noa. It's Chris. He gestures at me to take the headphones off and he doesn't even mention the fact that I've been crying.

'Look, mate, I get it,' he says. 'I *know* how rough things can be. And the way I figure it, you've got to take what you can, when you can. Because no one else is going to help. You've got to make your own luck. Right?'

And the weird thing is that his eyes are kind of shining too.

I shrug.

'Come on! Just come with us, all right?' he asks. 'Look, don't make me beg! See . . . *you* know what it's like. Zayn doesn't, Charlie doesn't – *none* of that lot do. They just like acting up – they're all along for the ride – but *they* don't know what it's *really* like – you know, for people like you and me.'

And that's what does it.

In that moment, with the sun setting and his eyes glinting with tears, Chris has just said what I've been suspecting – we're kind of the same. I look over at him, my resolve wavering.

'So what? You're coming?' he asks, his arm draped over my shoulder, his eyebrows raised.

'Yeah,' I say eventually. 'I'll come.'

CHAPTER TWENTY-SEVEN

DO YOU EVER FEEL LIKE YOU'RE being led down a certain path? Like every choice you make decides your *future* choices too? And if you make one too many *bad* decisions, then that's it – you'll be trapped there in *that* life. *For ever.*

I guess that's what people mean when they talk about a slippery slope. And right now I get it – I feel like my feet are skidding about all over the place.

The station in our town's small. Basically there are two platforms, one going each way and there's no gates, so you don't need to buy a ticket before you get on a train. Which is just as well, all things considered.

We all walk in through the gate. Zayn's in front, with everyone else kind of drifting along behind, then me and Chris at the back. I don't know what it is but everyone seems really keyed up for some reason. There's this weird edgy atmosphere. I mean, even more so than usual.

'Don't worry about a ticket,' says Chris, 'they *never* check on this route, and at the other end we just jump the gates – it'll be fine. None of the guards really care either way – besides, they're all old – they're not going to bother sweating it out chasing us!'

'Right,' I say, nodding, 'but where are you going?'

'*We* . . .' says Chris, grinning as he pats me on the shoulder, 'where are *we* going? Magical mystery tour, isn't it?' He laughs. 'Come on! It'll be a laugh, all right?'

I shake my head slightly, but even though I could *easily* turn back, for some reason I don't.

We go and sit on these two benches, everyone talking so loudly that this young couple who were sitting on the one next to us, pick up their stuff and move away.

'What a loser,' says Zayn, spitting on the ground near the guy's feet. He must be in his mid-twenties and is pretty big – I'd say he goes to the gym and everything – but all the same he looks properly nervous.

And I know I should just leave now. Really, I *know* I should, but I just don't feel like I *can*. Do you know those old Scalextric tracks? Where you race toy cars round a course by pulling a trigger and all you can do is choose how fast you go? *That's* what I feel like. Like all I can do is speed up and up and up until *eventually* I'll spin out and get thrown off on a corner. The only question is *when*.

I see the train approaching down the line and just then I hear my name called. I look round, over to the other side of the track.

It's Kalia. She's with Lani. They're looking over at me. At me hanging out with Chris, Zayn and all the others. What if she's spoken with Noa? What if he's told her about the headphones going missing just after I was in his shop with Chris? I want to gesture that this isn't me. Not *really*. That I'm *stuck*, that I can't get away. But I can't speak at all. I just freeze, looking blankly over, like I don't know them at all.

Kalia's saying something to Lani and his brows are furrowed. Kalia's eyes are wide now; she's beckoning me over.

'*Will!*' she shouts as the train pulls in. 'Come on! Come over here!'

But I can't. I just *can't*. My feet aren't working. My brain's not working. The train thunders into the station, rumbling between us, cutting her off and suddenly I can breathe again.

The blur of lights on the train becomes a staccato stutter of windows, doors and bored-looking commuters waiting to get off. Then it stops and Zayn elbows his way on board, followed by everyone else.

'Come on, Will,' says Chris, his hand resting on my shoulder, pushing me gently forward. 'Let's get a move on.'

On the train I completely avoid looking towards Kalia and Lani, but I can feel them both watching me. As the train pulls out of the station, I feel a ripping sensation inside me as I move away from my old life. And I *know* that Kalia's still watching me. I can feel her eyes on me even when the station's completely out of view.

'Hey, Poundland!' calls Zayn, way louder than he needs to in the busy carriage. 'Wasn't that your girlfriend?'

The other lads laugh until Chris glares at them. 'You going to be a tool your whole life, Zayn? Give Will a break, right?'

Everyone goes quiet, waiting to see how Zayn responds. His cheeks flush slightly and I can see his knuckles whiten, but a second or two later he half smiles and says, 'Take it easy, Chris! I'm just having a laugh!'

'Glad to hear it,' replies Chris, half smiling back as he stares directly into Zayn's eyes. 'We're all mates here, *right*?'

'Yeah, course,' replies Zayn, shrugging, still doing that cold empty smile.

After a while, things settle down a bit and everyone starts chatting. I get out my headphones and am about to put them on when Chris moves over next to me.

'You did the right thing back there,' he says. 'Girls just complicate things. You get me?'

I don't. I don't get him. I don't know what I'm doing here, or where we're even going, but I nod all the same. Then I put my headphones on and lean my forehead against the window, peering out into the night, at the tiny pinpricks of light that slide past in the huge ocean of darkness.

CHAPTER TWENTY-EIGHT

'OKAY, SO, NICE AND CASUAL ON the walk-up,' says Chris. He sounds calm but his eyes are gleaming with an electric light and I can see a vein throbbing in his neck. 'Then when you're at the gate, just vault it. Up and over! We all do it at the same time and they're stuffed! They can't chase *all* of us – they won't even have time to shout. Yeah?'

I nod but my stomach's churning. We're only forty-five minutes away from home, but this place is totally different. The station here is massive.

All shiny metal, expensive coffee shops and bars everywhere, with escalators leading up to the main shopping area. There are six gates in a row and we all fan out. Charlie's got his skateboard with him and Chris nudges me. 'Keep an eye on Charlie,' he says. 'He's got, like, a *signature* move . . .'

We're almost at the gate now. My heart's pounding. Charlie is grinning to himself, and all of a sudden he throws his skateboard down and dives forward, landing on the deck on his belly and shooting under the ticket barrier. His momentum carries him forward at least five metres, then he's up and running, skateboard under one arm, laughing wildly.

'Now!' yells Chris.

Everything goes in slow motion. My hands are on the gates. I fling myself up, feet scrambling over the metal. I smack my elbow on the gate and fall down the other side, almost slipping over, but Chris grabs me and heaves me up.

'Up you get!' he yells, eyes gleaming.

Then we're running.

I can hear the station workers shouting, but I don't look back. I just run. I've never run so fast, so hard, and it feels *amazing*. Total freedom, letting everything go. Like in that moment all the weight's been taken away and I just feel this pure exhilaration. I'm laughing, and

Chris is laughing, the sound ringing behind us as we sprint out of the station.

A few minutes later, and we've met up with everyone again. We're walking down some narrow road near a row of rotting old brickwork arches, all damp and forgotten about. It's exactly the kind of place that people come to do things that they don't want to be seen.

'Time to get down to business,' says Chris, looking round at the group. 'Basically none of you lot say anything. *All right?* Just leave it all to me. These lads aren't messing about, so, everyone, keep it shut, okay?' He glances over at Zayn, whose mouth curls up into a sneer.

'Right . . . so we just sit behind you like good little boys, and you do all the talking?'

I can feel that weird air again, like everyone's waiting to see how Chris will respond, waiting to see if there's going to be a sudden shift in dynamics.

'*Gosh, Zayn,*' says Chris, voice dripping in sarcasm, 'it's like you actually *understand*! Well done. You get a gold star, *mate!*'

Zayn glares at Chris but doesn't say anything and eventually looks away.

No one else seems to notice but I see Chris exhale slowly.

'Okay . . .' he says, 'they'll be here any minute, so at least try to ACT like you know what you're doing. *All right?*'

I watch as everyone nods. I probably even nod myself.

A couple of minutes later, a group of lads walk towards us from the other end of the street. It's the same group I'd seen under the bridge by the river near Mum's. Si, Tony, Mo and all his other mates. They don't say anything. Si just gestures down one of the tunnels with his head and they walk on.

Chris looks round at us all, his jaw set, his breathing shallow. 'Come on then!' he hisses. 'We're not here to mess about!'

Water drips from the archway above, quiet drops tapping the lichen-covered slabs as we walk along the musty tunnel. No one says anything. Zayn's swinging his arms like he's some sort of gorilla. Chris is leading the way, his face hard and cold. A few metres ahead, Si and the others are standing in a beam of murky light filtering down from dirty glass blocks in the pavement above our heads.

'Baby Tucker,' he says, almost smiling. 'I see you brought your boys along? *Scary!*'

'Don't push it!' spits Zayn.

Chris's eyes widen. I don't even really see Si moving; it's like one moment he's standing there nonchalantly, and the next he's got his fists round Zayn's top, nose to nose, holding him up against the filthy wall.

'Nah, mate,' he says. 'That's *not* how we do things.'

Zayn's eyes are bulging as Si flings him to the ground where he sprawls out all tangled up in the rubbish.

Si glares down, while Zayn shuffles awkwardly to his feet. 'You going to behave?'

Zayn nods and goes to stand behind Chris, his tracksuit bottoms ripped and mud streaked across his top.

Si rubs a hand across his forehead. 'You need to have

a word with that one, Chris,' he says.

'Yeah, will do. Sorry, mate,' says Chris.

For a moment Si just stares at him. 'So how did you do?' he asks eventually.

'Pretty good,' replies Chris. 'I got loads of the things you'd asked for. I even got those headphones.' He glances over at me for a second here. '*And* the phones. Couldn't get the perfume, though.'

Chris bends down and opens his rucksack, pulling out a whole bunch of brand-new boxed electronics and handing it all over to Si.

Time slows down again. No one says anything; we're all just watching Si.

After what feels like ages, he nods to himself. Reaching into his jacket, he pulls out an envelope, peers into it, puts in another twenty and throws it over to Chris, who catches it and nods, putting it in his pocket.

'Well, it looks like we're done!' says Si, turning away. 'See you later, Baby Tucker.'

'Wait a minute . . .' says Chris. 'Any of you lads

interested in something else?'

Si laughs. 'You're good value!' he says. 'Go on then, what have you got in mind?'

Chris walks forward with his bag and holds it open so Si can look in.

'You're a right little wheeler-dealer,' says Si, laughing, 'but I'm all right, cheers!' He gestures down to his feet, and I see that he's got the same trainers that Cameron had, just in a different colour scheme.

'Fair play, you've got some stones,' he says, grinning. 'I'll have to keep an eye on you!'

I look over at Chris and it's like he's swollen to about twice his size. He's smiling, like, a real happy smile, as though he's forgotten all about the front, all about being hard, and in that moment he just looks like a kid desperate for approval.

'Now, go on, get lost,' says Si, nodding down the far end of the tunnel. As we all walk off, he catches Chris's arm.

'Good work, Baby Tucker. I'll be in touch, yeah?'

CHAPTER TWENTY-NINE

WE ALL WALK DOWN THE TUNNEL.
It feels like it stretches on for ever.

None of the other lads says a word. All of them are making out like this is *totally* normal, but I can *feel* their combined adrenaline, the electric charge in the air.

Charlie starts whistling under his breath, swinging his skateboard casually, then obviously realises it seems weird and stops. A few more steps and we're out of the tunnel and round the corner – away from that claustrophobic atmosphere, away from Si and those older lads.

The nervous energy that was crackling around the tunnel explodes. They all start jostling each other, slapping each other on the back and laughing, all talking at the same time.

'OH MY GOD!' explodes Chris, looking round at us all, his eyes like Os. 'Just look at THIS!' He pulls out that envelope and opens it up, fanning out more money than I've ever seen in one place.

'SHUT UP!' says Charlie. 'How much is there?'

'Dunno,' says Chris, flicking through the notes. 'I'd say roughly . . . A LOT!'

'Sick!'

'That's insane, mate!'

'Tell you what, though,' says Zayn, 'that kiddie's going to get a slap if he tries anything like that again!'

'Yeah, RIGHT!' says Charlie. 'You looked like you was going to cry when he chucked you on the floor!'

'Leave it out!' says Chris, shaking his head. 'Come on, look at this!' He holds up the money. 'We're *minted*! And you *all* helped, so everyone gets a bit, right?' He looks at me. 'Well, not you Will – that one was kind of a test, but you can be in on the next run, if you like?' He says it casually but I can see everyone turn to look at me.

Things go a bit quiet as Chris is counting out the money and passing it round to everyone. 'Come on then!' says Chris. 'Let's hear it? Are you with us?'

I say nothing.

Zayn's sort of smirking but he's careful not to let Chris see.

'I dunno,' I say.

'Come on! It's *easy* money!' says Chris. He gestures at the notes in his hand; it's probably enough to sort out the situation with Damien Forsyth *and* to get us sorted for the next few weeks.

And you know what? I *could* do it. It would be easy. I could just not ask any questions, do what I'm told and take the money. I *really* could.

But . . . I dunno. It's just not *me*, you know? I mean, Cameron would *totally* give up on me – Kalia too – and I'd have keep it all from Dad. It would mean SO many secrets, so many lies.

'*Come on, Will!*' urges Chris in a low voice, grabbing hold of my arm. 'I vouched for you. I'm doing you a *favour* here! Just think, this could sort you *right* out.'

The weird thing is that I really think he wants us to be friends. Like he knows that we connect in some way. And he's right: we kind of do. Or at least we understand each other. But like *this*? Is that really what I want?

I look at him, his brows raised, head nodding slightly.

'I'm *bored*!' says Zayn. 'Leave it, Chris – he's a waste of space!'

'*Shut up*, Zayn!' hisses Chris, almost baring his teeth, then he turns back to me. 'How about it, Will?'

I've got no idea what I'm going to say. As I open my mouth to speak, I see a silvery white blur streak out from one of the railway arches nearby. A huge gleaming bird with an impossibly large wingspan, a sharp curved beak and fierce talons trailing behind.

'What the hell is *that*!?' yells Zayn as the owl sweeps through the air behind him.

Settling on an old telegraph pole nearby, the owl stares down at me, its piercing eyes seeming to know everything that I've ever done, everything I ever *will* do – every good thing, every bad thing – but I don't feel afraid.

In those eyes there's no judgement, just understanding, because life *is* hard, and sometimes we make the wrong choices. But that doesn't mean that you can't also make the *right* choices.

That's the power that we *all* have in any given moment, the power to make one decision or another. And you've *got* to make the best decision that you can with what you've got to hand.

I don't know how long it all lasts, seconds probably, but it feels much longer. Then the owl stretches its wings and takes off, soaring up into the cold night sky – fierce, wild and free – totally independent.

I know exactly what I'm going to say.

CHAPTER THIRTY

'SORRY, CHRIS,' I SAY, MY VOICE an ocean of calm. 'It's just not for me.'

The pounding that was in my chest, my ears and my throat has fallen away. I don't feel at all scared right now. I just *know* that whatever may or may *not* happen as a result, this isn't the right choice for me. So I can't do it.

Chris looks at me for a second. His eyes wide. He looks stunned, hurt almost, like I've just punched him in the face. But almost immediately that look hardens. Any vulnerability shatters and beneath it the harsh cold mask that I recognise as his face is revealed.

'I should have known . . .' he whispers under his breath. 'I should have *known* you'd be no use!' He pushes me lightly backwards with his fingertips, his mood darkening. Zayn and the others look over, excited – the air thickening, darkening.

'Fine!' he shouts. '*Fine!* Piss off back to Poundland! Go on! Crawl back under your rock in Cherry Orchards and live your nothing life! I gave you a chance, though. Remember that! I *tried* to help you!'

He turns round, gesturing to Zayn and the others to leave. Then he spins back, eyes narrowed, and I can't believe that I ever saw anything other than hate in him. 'Hey, boys, check out Poundland's weird music thing!' he spits.

One by one they all gather round me, a toxic cocktail of bad aftershave, jittery nervous energy and the potential for violence.

'Go on, then!' barks Zayn. 'Show us.'

I take the Walkman out of my pocket and hold it in front

of me slightly. Zayn reaches out and grabs it, pressing a bunch of random buttons and the music comes out way too fast, sounding high and squeaky.

'What you got on there? The Chipmunks or something?' asks Chris.

Everyone laughs.

'It's on fast-forward, but you've not pressed it all the way down,' I say quietly, but they're not listening. Someone else grabs it and tries to do the same thing, but now it's doing it in reverse. They all take turns messing about with it, grabbing it from each other and laughing.

'Leave it out,' I say. 'It'll chew up the tape.'

'Whatever,' replies Chris, dropping the Walkman to the ground like he's bored of that game now. It sits there, the wheels spinning round but no sound coming out of the headphones.

Chris looks at me, a strange sort of light shining darkly in his eyes. He's about to say something, I can tell. Then he nods down at my shoes. 'Those shoes are a joke, Poundland.'

I shrug. There is literally *nothing* I can say to defend my shoes.

'How d'you fancy getting your hands on something a bit better?'

I look over at him as the other boys glance round at each other, sort of sniggering. 'What do you mean?'

'Think of me like some kind of Robin Hood,' says Chris. 'You know? Robbing from the rich to give to the poor.'

I don't know what he's on about and, to be honest, I don't really care. All I want now is to get out of here. To get back home. To get back to who I *used* to be. Who I *really* am. I feel tired. Tired of hanging around in this grimy backstreet, tired of the whole thing.

A flicker of irritation runs across his face. He seems annoyed that I'm not playing along – that I'm not scared.

Shrugging his rucksack off his shoulder, Chris opens the zip and pulls out a pair of trainers. They're black mesh with a gold tick and this thin flexible panel on the side where you can upload whatever graphics, and even videos, if you like, from your phone.

They're Cameron's trainers.

'They're Cameron's trainers,' I say kind of stupidly.

'They're yours if you want them,' says Tucker. 'Fifty quid and they're yours.' Now, for a minute my brain does this weird thing where it tries to calculate how cool it would be to have those shoes, offset with the fact that I could never wear them anywhere because everybody would *know* I'd basically stolen them, and then finally subtracted from that is the fact that Cameron's my best mate, so even if I *could* get away with it, I wouldn't *want* to.

'Ha! *Look!*' says Chris. 'He's trying to work out where he can get the money from! We've got a bite. Now all we've got to do is reel him in . . .'

Something inside me goes cold at that moment. Even if I *wanted* to, I couldn't get my hands on fifty pounds without, I don't know, robbing a corner shop or something.

Suddenly I'm angry. All the resentment I feel from every little humiliation I go through on a daily basis rises up through me and takes over. You know what, I don't care any more. But not in the same way as before. Because now I don't care about Chris and his stupid mates. I don't care what they *might* do. They seem small and desperate the way they're all scrambling about, looking for approval, trying to feel powerful – it's pathetic.

I smile. I *actually* smile, which I don't think anyone was expecting. I certainly wasn't. I look Chris up and down. That's when I notice that his feet are kind of tiny. Ordinarily I'd never even notice that sort of thing, let alone comment on it, but I feel in this case it's fair game.

'No, Chris,' I say slowly. 'I was just wondering what sort of an *idiot* steals a pair of shoes that's too big for them.'

Everything goes quiet. Tucker looks at me, his face a swirling sea of emotions – at first surprised, then upset and then angry. I stand there, waiting for something awful to happen. But the funny thing is, sometimes life isn't as bad as you think it's going to be.

'Yeah, well, *whatever*!' spits Chris. 'It's not like *you'd* have the nerve! Besides, I'd never have sold them to you for *fifty quid*. You think I'm stupid? I'll get loads more online. You wait. And don't bother telling anyone; it's just your word against mine. And really? Who's going to listen to a loser like *you*?' He steps towards me suddenly, raising his fist quickly and I flinch. He and his friends all laugh as he shoves me hard and I fall over backwards, sprawling on the ground.

Zayn runs over towards me, fists raised, his eyes gleaming with an awful darkness.

'Leave it!' says Chris, pulling him back. 'He's not worth

it. Come on, let's get out of here.' Then he kicks my Walkman hard, sending it skidding over the pavement and smashing into the wall.

'See you around, Poundland!' he spits, then they all turn and leave.

Slowly I pick myself up, breathing heavily. The adrenaline is flooding through me, my legs literally shaking. When I walk over to pick up the Walkman, the plastic's cracked, the batteries have come out, the tape is all chewed up and the front tape slot is totally broken. I shove all the broken pieces in the front pocket of my bag, zip it up and then I walk away.

CHAPTER THIRTY-ONE

IN ALL SERIOUSNESS I THOUGHT
I was going to have to beg to get the money for the train
ride home. But as luck would have it, there was a problem
with the gates and all the station workers were just
waving everyone through. There'd been a cancellation
or something, so the train was rammed and I had to sit
on the floor outside the toilet along with a whole bunch
of other people. It smelled *properly* grim, but on the plus
side there was no ticket collector wandering up and
down, so I had no problems getting home.

As I walk towards our flat, I see Dad leaning against the front door, peering out into the night. He's chatting on the phone.

'*Wait!* No . . . Look, don't worry. It's okay. He's here now. Sorry, Abi, I'll call you back in a bit, all right? And thanks again. For *everything*. Yep. Yep . . . Cheers then. Bye now.'

He turns to face me, his face pale, hands raised up. 'Will!' he exclaims. 'I've been going *mad*! When you didn't come home, I just didn't know what had –' he shakes his head, eyes wide and gleaming – 'me, your mum and Greg have been *all over* looking for you. I thought you'd run away or worse . . . *What happened? Where have you been?*'

I take a deep breath, hold it in for a moment and then slowly I begin to let it all out. Not just my breath. But *everything*.

I tell Dad the truth. How desperate I've been feeling recently. About the row with Cameron, about Chris, about the headphones I stole, about *everything*.

'The thing is . . .' I say as we sit down on the sofa, hands cradled round warm cups of tea, 'I just feel like everything's out of my control . . . Like I don't have a *choice*!'

'But you *do*!' insists Dad. 'Don't you see? That's what you did tonight! When you told those lads that you wouldn't steal anything else for them.'

'I suppose . . .'

'There's no *suppose* about it!' insists Dad. 'You *always*

have a choice. And *that* choice –' he looks me right in the eyes – 'the one that you just made, would have been a tough one. It's always easier to just go along with the crowd. You were brave back there, Will. I'm proud of you.' He nods, eyes shining as he pulls me into a hug. 'I *really* am.'

Sometimes that sort of thing can embarrass me a bit, but right now it feels the best – warm, safe and secure.

'You were right by the way,' he says after a moment.

'About what?'

'About Damien Forsyth,' says Dad, shaking his head. 'I should never have had anything to do with him.' He looks down. 'I'm not proud of myself. I know that I put us both at risk and I'm sorry.'

I try to protest. 'It's all right—'

Dad shakes his head. 'But it's *not*. I'm your dad! I'm the one who's meant to look out for *you* – not the other way round.' He looks at me, and, sure, he still looks thin, he still looks older, but there's something in his eyes that I've not seen for a long time – they've got some light back, some energy. 'And *look* . . . you don't need to worry about Damien. Your mum and Greg lent me the money to pay him back, and a bit extra to tide us over . . .' He shakes his head. 'I mean, that's NOT the way I wanted this to play out, but sometimes you've just got to accept some help – even if it *hurts*.'

I let out the breath that I hadn't even realised I'd been holding from somewhere deep within me. Good old Mum, good old Greg! I mean, I know that Dad's going to hate owing them money, but it's *got* to be better than owing it to Damien.

'Look, I was thinking . . .' I say, 'perhaps I could help you with the odd jobs? You know, we'd get the money to pay them back quicker then?'

Dad's face brightens. 'Well, *actually*, there's a bit of good news on the old job front. Remember that one that I went for? The one I thought I'd got? Well, they've had *another* role up at the same place, and I only went and got it! I mean, it's part-time so it's not loads of money, but still, it's a damn sight more than we've had recently.'

'Seriously?'

Dad nods. 'Seriously.'

My eyes are stinging, my vision blurred behind refracted rainbows of light in the tears that are forming. He's got a job – an *actual* job.

'I reckon there's a good chance for a promotion too,' says Dad, winking as he nudges me with one elbow. 'Give it a couple of months, I'll be CEO.'

'Come on, don't get all overexcited again!' I say, grinning as I shove his elbow away.

'*I won't! I won't!*' counters Dad, grinning too. 'But I've got a good feeling about this.'

I laugh because what else can I do? I laugh out of relief, I laugh because of the daft face that he's pulling, and I laugh because the light that's been rekindled in his eyes seems to be saying that perhaps this time things *are* going to be different.

Then we cook dinner together and I do the washing-up while Dad chooses a DVD for us to watch and it feels nice. You know? Normal. Real. *Safe.*

CHAPTER THIRTY-TWO

THE NEXT MORNING, I WAKE UP early, feeling a whole load lighter than I have in ages. I think I might *actually* have slept a decent amount last night. I get out of bed and walk through to the kitchen, calling Dad to see if he's up yet.

He's not around but there's a note on the table.

Gone to work! Not written that in a while . . .

BTW I got your Walkman fixed last night. You might not be able to teach an old dog new tricks, but I can still do all the old tricks pretty well!

D X

Good old Dad. I pick the Walkman up and turn it over in my hands, smiling. He's done an amazing job, considering what a mess it was in. I mean, it still looks battered but it *seems* to be working. I press the play button down and the wheels turn. I fast-forward, then rewind. Everything's doing what it's meant to do. I grin.

I fix myself some porridge then I head out of the house into the cold fresh morning. I breathe into my cupped hands, wishing that I still had that hat. I never *did* get it back and my ears are freezing! I slide the retro headphones over my ears, grateful for even that little bit of protection from the wind, and press play.

My heart does this sort of jolting flip. I don't hear any

music. I hear talking instead. And not just *any* talking, I hear Chris Tucker and me talking.

Well . . . *now* my heart's really going for it. Someone must have pressed the record button while they were messing about with the Walkman last night. I hear Chris saying how he'd stolen the trainers. I hear me calling him an idiot. *Me* calling *him* an idiot. It's pretty world-changing stuff, to be honest. As I listen to myself standing up to him, it makes me think about *everything* differently. You know, in that moment *I won*. And yeah, sure, Chris and his mates sort of ended up on top. But right *then* I was winning. I smile as I realise I'm not scared of him any more. He's got no power over me.

And not only that. I've got *proof* he stole Cameron's trainers.

Then I have an idea, and do you know what? I think it might even be the best idea that I've ever had in my life. I walk into school, smiling all the way, glad that I'm going to be early for once.

After everyone's settled down and finally stopped

chattering, the head strolls out in front of us all, like every time he does an assembly. After he's done the basic meet and greet, he tells us about how we're going to listen to a piece today that is truly enlightening, a piece that clearly denotes the triumph of the human spirit.

I sit there, grinning madly, a whole greenhouse worth of butterflies jittering around in my stomach. This lad from Year Ten's sat next to me, looking over, all curious as to why I'm so wired.

'*What?*' he whispers.

'*Nothing . . .*' I reply, literally biting my lip to keep quiet.

The head presses the clicker and the slide changes. He closes his eyes, as he always does, and waits for the music to build up around him. Except, of course, it doesn't.

There's no music playing at all.

What comes out over the PA is talking.

The head sits up, looking around, confused, as everyone listens to Chris Tucker talking to me about how he stole Cameron's shoes – the whole thing, *including* the bit where I call him a small-footed idiot.

Everyone laughs. It's glorious, like a thousand suns all rising and setting at the same time, throwing dazzling beams of light around the inside of my head. Then it gets to the bit where he says, 'And don't bother telling anyone; it's just your word against mine. And really? Who's going to listen to a loser like *you*?'

Well, that does it. The murmuring that's been going round the hall erupts and everyone's suddenly standing up, looking around to see if they can see either me or Chris Tucker.

'*Will!* That was *immense*!' yells Cameron from a couple of rows back. He's grinning at me, his eyes wild

and bright. People are all over me, patting me on the back, you know, real scoring-the-winning-goal-in-the-last-seconds-of-the-match sort of stuff. The teachers are trying to calm it all down, when Chris does this crazy kamikaze dash to the doors to try to get out, but Mr Pugh, Mr Prince and Miss Taylor make a barricade to stop him. It's absolute madness for a while and takes *loads* of shouting from Mrs Fairweather to get it all under control, but the whole time everyone's smiling at me. Even the head catches my eye and does this little wink. I mean, it's kind of weird seeing the head wink at you, but, you know what, I'll take it. I'll take feeling good over feeling bad.

'But how did you do it?' asks Cameron after everything's calmed down a bit and we're heading over to our next lesson.

I shrug. 'I've done enough detentions to know how to set up the files for assembly,' I say, 'and it was just a case of getting the recording from my Walkman on to the school computer. No big deal really. Although the head *did* say that if I ever did anything like that again, I'd be in BIG trouble.' I grin. 'Still, I thought I'd be in big trouble for doing this – so, all in all, I think I got off lightly!'

I stop and turn to Cameron. 'Look, mate, I want to say sorry—'

'Don't worry about it,' says Cameron, shaking his head and sort of looking away.

'No. I *need* to say this,' I explain. 'Look, I *know* you were only looking out for me. And I was acting like an idiot. It's hard to explain, but I was in a *properly* bad place, you know? But everything feels better now. So, yeah, I just wanted to say sorry because . . . because I am.'

Cameron nods. 'Yeah, well . . . *I* need to say sorry too.' He shakes his head. 'You know what? You're right . . . I didn't get it.' He pauses. 'To be honest, I still don't *really* get it – how things are for you – but I do want to *try* to. You know? You're my best mate, *right*?'

'Absolutely,' I say, draping my arm over his shoulder.

'I've also got kind of a confession to make . . .' says Cameron.

I glance over at him, eyebrows raised.

'Yeah . . .' he says, 'well, you know Omari Samuels in your Art class?'

I nod. Of course I do.

'He told me about what you did with your painting . . .' He pauses again, like he's worried about something. 'You know, ripping it all up and that . . . So I kind of taped it together?' He holds out his phone and shows me a photo of the painting. That painting of an owl, filled with life and energy and hope, which had been torn up and crushed, and now repaired.

My eyes sting with tears. Because of *course* you can still see the joins and the white seams of the rip marks scored through the paint, but you know what? If anything, that just improves it. That makes it more real somehow – because nobody makes it through life without getting a *bit* damaged at some point or other.

Cameron looks at me, twisting his fingers together. 'And while I was in the art room, Mr Prince came back from his doctor's appointment, and he kind of . . . well, you know . . .'

'What?'

'He . . . sort of helped me enter it into the competition for you?' says Cameron, half looking away. 'You're not cross, are you?'

'*No way!*' I say, laughing. 'That's amazing! Thanks, Cameron!' And I pull him into a hug – a real tight *best-mates* hug.

'Awww! Well, isn't *that* a heart-warming scene?' says Kalia, walking over. 'Look at you two!'

'Leave it out, Kalia!' I say, trying to sound casual, but I feel this huge wave of relief that she's still talking to me.

She smiles at me and I grin back.

'Hey, Kalia. Look, I know that I've been a bit weird recently—'

'What on earth do you mean?' she interrupts. 'You mean when you totally blanked me at the station and made me look like an idiot? Or perhaps you mean when you—'

'Yeah, well . . . any of it,' I say. 'Look, I'm sorry, okay? For all of it!'

'Well, I forgive you,' she says, gesturing at me like she's some kind of queen. 'Now stop grovelling – it's demeaning!'

I grin, then my face falls. There's still something that I need to do – but I *really* don't want to. No one *ever* wants to do anything hard.

I look between Kalia and Cameron, that sick feeling twisting up inside me again. 'So . . . I've got something to say, and I *think* when I tell you it's going to change how you feel about me . . .' I pause. This is *impossible*. Here they are, my best friends, and what I'm about to say could well change all that. It's something that could throw me back on to that dark path, where I felt completely alone. But, *come on*, if you can't tell your best friends the truth, what kind of friendship do you actually have?

They're looking at me, faces all worried, eyes wide, waiting . . .

'There's no easy way to say this . . .' I start, then I stop again. And when I finally start speaking, the words pour out like a waterfall.

'See, the thing is, I stole some headphones. From GameXchange –' I glance at Kalia – 'your brother's shop. And I didn't know it was his shop at the time, not like that makes it any better, but I swear I *didn't*! And anyway, I felt awful about it – I *feel* awful about it. And it wasn't for me or anything; it was for Chris to give to these other lads, but all the same I still did it. I was just . . . you know, in a really bad place. There was all his stuff going on with my dad and this loan shark and . . . and . . . and I felt like I didn't have a choice. Like I didn't have *any* choices. But now I can see that I did – and I'm sorry . . .' I pause. 'And I'll repay him. I *promise* I will. As soon as I can.'

I look at them, expecting to see their eyes harden, to grow cold. Expecting them to walk away.

'You know what?' says Kalia. 'My brother did say that some little "scrote", as he put it, had stolen some headphones yesterday.' She looks at me, her eyebrows dipping in the middle. 'I'd never have guessed it was *you*, though!'

Cameron just looks totally shocked, like I've told him that I'm actually an alien or something. For a while nobody says anything.

My face feels like the skin on it's going to burn up and peel away. If they're going to turn their backs on me and walk away, I just want them to do it now – let's get this over with.

Then Kalia shrugs. 'Still, you've told me now –' she pauses – 'and if you're going to pay for the headphones at some point, then I guess it's just like one of those buy-now-pay-later kind of deals.'

'So . . . so you're not angry?'

'Angry?' says Kalia, shaking her head. 'No, I'm not *angry*, Will. Surprised? Yes. But not angry. The thing is, I guess I can see how you might get into a mess like that.' Her lips pull back slightly into a lopsided smile. 'I mean, *I* wouldn't, of course, but I can kind of see how *YOU* might!'

Cameron snorts out a laugh and Kalia grins at him.

Relief floods through me. This is way more than I deserve and I know it.

'So is that it?' I ask, looking at them both. 'Are we good?'

'I hope so,' says Kalia and she's properly smiling now, 'otherwise you might record some of our private conversations and broadcast them to the whole school.' She elbows me in the ribs, hard. 'Fair play, Will – that was something else.' She looks over to Cameron. 'So you're Cameron, right?'

Cameron nods. 'Yeah.'

'Thought so. Will's told me *all* about you.'

'He has?' asks Cameron, eyebrows dancing upwards.

'*No!*' replies Kalia, snorting out a laugh. 'As if! He's *totally* self-absorbed. But he did say he had a friend called Cameron, and I don't think he's got any *other* friends, so I put two and two together!'

Cameron laughs. I laugh. We all laugh. And, just like that, everything's changed. I've gone from feeling lost, like I'm invisible, like everything's broken and I'm totally alone, to *this* – being here, right now, laughing with my friends.

Although, when you look at it, nothing's *really* changed in my life, apart from how I feel about it. I guess that's one of those funny things about life – it's about how you *feel* about what's happening, as much as the actual events.

And right now I'm feeling pretty good.

'WILL! HEY, WILL! WAIT UP!'

It's Chris Tucker's voice. I'd know it anywhere.

I close my eyes for a moment, take a deep breath, then turn round. To tell the truth, this is the last thing I need right now. Since Dad got his new job, I've taken over as Mrs Robinson's handyman. I've been doing odd jobs round at hers all day and I'm pretty much wiped out.

'Look, Chris . . .' I say, glancing over at him quickly, 'I don't want any hassle, all right?'

'Neither do I!' says Chris, raising his hands in a

310

frustrated gesture. 'Why does *everyone* always think I'm looking for trouble?'

I raise one eyebrow. I can think of at least nineteen reasons, but I don't think listing them all right now would be a great idea. 'So what do you want?'

He stands there a moment, saying nothing, grinding the ground with his foot. He looks different now, all the swagger's gone, and without that it's hard to see what's left.

'You hear about Zayn and that lot?' he asks eventually.

I nod. 'They got caught breaking into a warehouse or something?'

'*Hardly!*' he mutters. 'It was more like the back room of a newsagent's, but, yeah, breaking and entering. Flashing lights, handcuffs, the whole deal. They'll be up in court before long.'

I whistle in through my teeth and shake my head. 'That's not great.'

Chris nods. 'Yeah, you're right there. See, that's the thing . . .' He pauses for a while, then almost winces.

'Go on,' I say. 'What is it?'

His eyes flick over towards me. He takes a deep breath, closes his eyes and shakes his head. 'It's not easy, is it?'

'*What's* not easy?'

He scowls and jabs a finger over towards me. 'This! And *you're* not making it any easier!'

'Look, I've got no idea what you're on about,' I reply, 'so if you've got something to say, just say it, all right? I'm tired and want to get home for some tea.'

It's weird, there's no way I'd have spoken to the *old* Chris like that. Old Chris Tucker with his gang of mates. But a lot can happen in a few weeks, and *new* Chris just doesn't scare me. To be honest, I feel a bit sorry for him.

After Chris got suspended, Zayn staged a coup and took over their little group, elbowing Chris out, leaving him all on his own, drifting around school like a lost soul. He's the new me, except people don't just ignore him; they *actively* dislike him. It's not hard to see why – over the years he's given grief to pretty much everyone.

'Look, I wanted to say thanks,' he blurts, '*all right?*'

'*Thanks?*' I repeat, staring at him. That is one hundred per cent NOT what I was expecting him to say.

'What for?'

'Couple of things . . .' he mutters. 'I mean, firstly, you could have told everyone about all the other stuff. You know, the stuff I'd picked up for Si and that.'

I shrug. 'Well, I did think about it,' I say. 'I probably should have done. Cameron and Kalia think I'm mad for keeping quiet about that. But it's complicated, right? That way, I'd have had to tell everyone that I stole those headphones too. I mean, I've paid Kalia's brother back now, so it's all sorted, but still . . .' I trail off. 'To be honest, I just want to put it all behind me.'

Chris nods. 'See, that's the other thing,' he says. 'I also wanted to say thanks for all of it. *Everything.* Playing the recording in school – nice touch by the way – getting me suspended. The whole lot.'

'You're thanking me for getting you suspended?' I stare at him. It's like he's reading from a totally different script to me.

'Well, yeah –' he shrugs – 'if you'd not done that, I'd probably have wound up going out with Zayn and Chris and breaking into that place too. I'd have spent a night in the cells and I'd be looking at a court date. I'd be on my way to messing *everything* up. The way I see it, I got off lightly, you know? Like I've got a second chance.'

I look at him. 'I guess everyone deserves at least one, right?'

'Right,' he says, nodding. 'And there's one more thing, while I'm doing all the feelings stuff . . . I wanted to say . . . well, I need to say sorry too. You know, for . . . well . . . for everything.'

It turns out we've not even got different scripts; he's ripped up both scripts and is totally freestyling. Now, I might be going mad here, but it seems like Chris has just apologised to me, and, to be honest, I'm not sure what to do with that. Of course, I *could* throw it back in his face. I could play some kind of power game here, just like he would have done a few weeks ago. I could hold that over him. Make him squirm, leave him hanging. Make him pay.

But I don't know . . . it really does seem like he's changed. Look, I'm not an idiot; it's not like I'd ever one hundred per cent trust him, but, like I say, everyone deserves at least *one* second chance. And besides, old Chris might have done something like that, but I never would have done. So I don't.

'Right,' I say, 'fair enough.'

'*Fair enough?*' Chris repeats. 'Is that all you've got to say?'

'What do you want?' I ask, turning to look him right in the eyes. 'You want me to tell you how you made my life miserable? How you and your mates crushed me and Cameron every single day just for fun? Just because you could? How you pushed us down so that you'd feel like *you* were rising up a little bit? I mean, yeah, sure . . . if *that's* what you want to hear, I can go into all that, because that's the truth of it. But seriously? What's the point? You know it. I know it, and if you're prepared to say sorry, I'm prepared to hear it. Okay? But it's not like I'm going to do a big "thank you so much" dance and give you a hug. Right?'

315

He looks at me. 'I suppose not . . .' Then he half smiles. 'But seriously, you don't want to do even a *little* bit of that dance? It sounds pretty sweet to me.'

I grin back at him. 'Sorry, Chris, but I save that dance for *very* special occasions.'

Chris nods. 'Sure, sure. I really do mean it, though. You know . . . *sorry.*'

'I know,' I reply, 'and, like I say, fair enough.'

'Right. Well, cheers then, Will.'

Chris starts to walk away. A few steps later he pauses and turns back. 'Look, you're probably not interested, but I got the new *Demonlance* game on the laptop. Maybe you could come over sometime and have a go on it?'

'Yeah, maybe . . .' I say. 'I've heard it's better than on mobile.'

'Way better!' he says, eyes lighting up. 'The graphics are *insane*. I got a couple of the miniatures with it too.'

'Seriously? You paint *Demonlance* miniatures?'

Chris shrugs. 'Well, not yet. I don't know how, but I'd like to give it a go.'

'I thought you hated all that D and D stuff?'

'Well, it's not exactly cool, is it?' he says. 'Zayn and the others would have ripped it out of me for sure.'

I nod. 'Yeah, I can see that. Besides, it's *way* cooler to get caught breaking into a newsagent's. Right?'

Chris laughs. 'Well, when you put it like that . . .'

And that's it. We're all done. Chris gives me his number and I tap it into my now fully dried out and revived phone, then he walks away down the street towards his place, and I carry on home to mine.

I suppose that this is that part where I wrap everything up and tell you how Dad got some amazing new promotion and we now live in a big house with a swimming pool and a games room and all that stuff, right?

Well, yeah . . . I could say all that, and if you're into wildly unrealistic endings, then you can just pretend that it's all true and stop reading now. Look, I'll even say 'THE END', if you like.

THE END.

There. All done!

But seriously? It's just *not* going to happen like that, is it? I mean, don't get me wrong, things are *way* better than they were, but it's not like my life's been transformed. See, the thing about life is that *bad* change can happen really quickly, but *good* change always seems slower. Just look at Zayn and that lot. One wrong move and suddenly everything's looking bleak, whereas me and Dad are grinding away, slowly climbing up out of that hole, trying to make things a little bit better each day. Sure, I'd love to wave a magic wand and instantly have no money problems at all, but so long as each day is a little bit better than the last – or at least not any worse – I'll take it.

Because that's the thing, when you're in a hole, then, like it or not, you've got to get yourself out. And yeah, it's not fair. I'm not saying it is. So, if you like, you can get all mad at the whole world and all the people who've never had anything but ladders and opportunities placed in front of them their whole life. But seriously, how does that help *you* get out of *your* hole?

Besides, if you're lucky, someone might offer you a

hand, try to show you the right route, give you a break, open some doors, but at the end of the day, for better or for worse, it's always *your* choice. You can always dig that hole deeper or try to climb out. And I know what *I* want to do.

Dad's still out when I get in, so I make some tea and toast, then I go through to my room. I put the plate and the mug down on the desk then I open my chest of drawers and there, right down at the bottom, underneath my T-shirts, all safely tucked away, is a small square envelope I made out of some thick card that Mr Prince gave me.

I take it out. The card's cool, crisp and firm in my fingers. Carefully I open it up and I smile.

Because there it is . . . a small perfect silvery feather that smells of wildness, freedom and the night sky.

And yeah, sure, I *know* I said that a little hope's a dangerous thing, but I'll tell you what . . .

It's better than none.

DEAR READER

THERE'S NO WAY TO SUGAR-COAT
this – *The Wrong Shoes* is a book which explores the crushing challenges facing children living in poverty. According to the Child Poverty Action Group, 4.2 million children were living in poverty in the UK in 2021/2022. That's one in three children who are going to struggle.

So, while *The Wrong Shoes* is a work of fiction, and Will is a made-up character, his general situation is most definitely not.

The trouble is that when your family is struggling,

it's hard to achieve even a baseline level of what you could be capable of, let alone anything more. It's hard to focus on lessons when you're tired, hungry, and worried about money. So, if the basics aren't covered, any extras like learning to play an instrument, buying the 'right' shoes, or having trips to the cinema are definitely not going to happen – you're always going to be at a disadvantage.

For children in Will's situation, there's always something blocking the way – obstacles that lots of other people never have to face and seem to walk right through.

It's Will's feeling of being disadvantaged that led to the title of the book. Will's dad can't afford to buy him the kind of trainers that the other kids have, and Will's own shoes are old and split on the sole – wrong in every possible way – an ugly, wet-footed reminder of the struggles he faces every day.

When I was young, my family didn't have much money for various reasons that are too complex to explain here, but even if it wasn't too long-winded to get into here, it would still be irrelevant.

After all, there is always a reason why a child is in a difficult financial situation. It may be because of a parent's alcoholism, addiction or mental health challenges – it might be all three. It could be due to a long-term illness in the family, or intergenerational poverty. It might be the result of a war, a house fire, an accident, or any sort of bad luck.

But one thing is certain – it is NEVER that child's fault. And yet, children like Will are still expected to just keep up with everyone else.

It is fundamentally unfair.

Of course, what's required here is more support for these children, more opportunities for them to learn, develop and eventually thrive. But sadly, that support framework is now less robust than it was when I was young, rather than more.

Will wants to work hard and to stay positive – but it's not easy. Nothing for Will is easy. But despite all these challenges and how they impact on Will's own mental health, I made the decision that with a bit of help and support, his sense of hope would never be fully diminished. Because while it IS all glaringly unfair, what's the alternative? To give up? Tempting as it sometimes seems, that's not going to help.

So, Will does all that he can do.

All that any of us can do when life gets hard – he picks himself up every time he falls over, trying to make the best choices available to him every single day.

And he keeps on going.

If this story resonates with you in any way at all, and things feel difficult right now, please, try to do the same thing.

TOM PERCIVAL

Tom Percival

is an author/illustrator who lives in Stroud with his family and The Best Dog in the World (apologies if you happen to think that your dog is The Best Dog in the World). A lot of his books explore social connections, community, equality and emotional growth, but he also makes room to write a bit of pure escapist fun once in a while. When he's not making books he enjoys walking/running around the countryside with The Best Dog in the World. He also makes music and enjoys taking photographs.

ACKNOWLEDGEMENTS

Thanks to everyone at Simon & Schuster for all of your hard-work and enthusiasm. Specifically to Lucy for telling me to expand a short story I had first written nearly seven years ago into the book you're now holding, Rachel for signing it off, and Michelle, David and Loren for all of your passion, skill, attention to detail and good humour. Without all those people, this book would either not exist, or if it did, it certainly wouldn't be as good. Thanks also to Mandy for all your time, help and energy and also for trying to ensure that I schedule my time in a vaguely sensible way. Finally, thanks to the National Literacy Trust, not only for supporting this book, but for everything that they do to improve outcomes for children across the UK.

National Literacy Trust

Change your story

Thank you for buying this copy of *The Wrong Shoes*.
£1 from your purchase has gone towards the vital work
of the National Literacy Trust, helping to empower
overlooked children to change their stories.

4.2 million children in the UK were living in
poverty in 2022 – that's one in three

Reading levels in children from disadvantaged
backgrounds are 20% lower than the national average

In 2022/23, the National Literacy Trust empowered
over 1.3 million children with the literacy skills they
need to shape their future. Every pound raised means
they can continue to work with communities that are
facing the biggest challenges with literacy. Together, we
are helping people change their stories.

Simon & Schuster Children's Books, Tom Percival
and the National Literacy Trust are working in
partnership on a campaign to deliver funds
and support, including:

A £1 donation to the National Literacy Trust
per hardback copy sold of *The Wrong Shoes*
before 1st May 2025

Book donations to all National Literacy Trust
priority communities – curated to reach the
needs of different age groups

National Literacy Trust regional community events
with Tom nationwide across the year, including a
nationally streamed public event

National press and events highlighting the
message of *The Wrong Shoes* and the work of
the National Literacy Trust

To find out more, visit www.literacytrust.org.uk

**National
Literacy
Trust**

Change your story